The

Handyman

www.BarbarianSpy.com

This book is copyright © habu
Published by BarbarianSpy in 2011
Cover design © S Bush 2011
Cover images: © Les3photo8 | Dreamstime.com
All rights reserved

ISBN: 978-1-921879-69-2

Published by BarbarianSpy an imprint of Cyberworld Publishing
Jindalee St, Toronto, Australia

Barbarian Spy

for Literary Heat

The

Handyman

by

habu

Shernhaven
Massachusetts

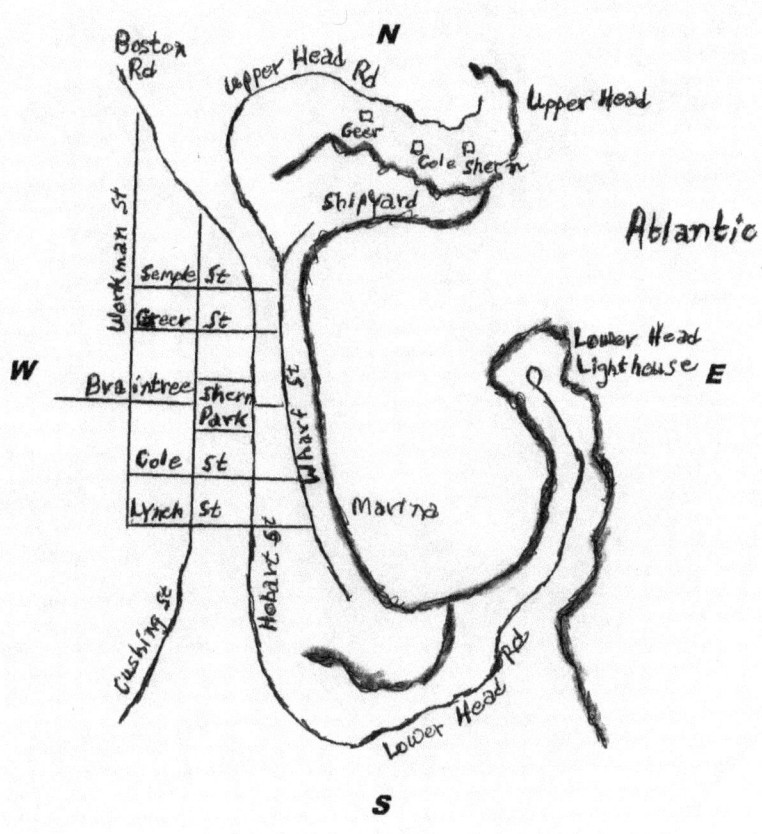

Prologue: 2010

The Trailways bus came in south from Boston on the Boston Road, turned right onto Cushing Street to come into Shernhaven on the east side of Shern Park, the center green of the old Massachusetts harbor town. Half way down the green it turned right again, headed east on Braintree Road and made an almost immediate turn left into the Shernhaven bus depot.

Only six passengers disembarked before the bus took on four more and headed east toward its next destination in Braintree.

The last one off the bus in Shernhaven was a young man of twenty-five or so in dusty jeans, a tight white T-shirt, and brown, ankle-high construction boots. He walked just a couple of paces down the curb toward the park from the door to the bus and bent over and placed a duffel bag and his jeans jacket on the ground. While he was straightening back up in a languid motion, he pulled a pack of cigarettes and matches from under the fold of the sleeve on one of his biceps. Cupping his hand over the flaring match and leaning his head down, he lit a cigarette between his lips.

He shook out the match and rather than tossing it on the ground, ran it into the hem of his jeans at one ankle. Taking several deep drags on the cigarette, he stood there and looked up and down Braintree Road, seemingly a stranger in town getting his bearings.

Standing in the window of the Union Bank of Norfolk directly across Braintree Road from the bus station, the bank's president, Trevor Cole, was taking the scenery in. He liked to have his desk near one of the front windows. He was a window shopper of sorts. And this young man who had gotten off the bus was just the sort of shopping Trevor Cole liked to do.

He found the young man quite attractive. Slender, but with a good build. He had an assuredness about him and a fluid movement that Cole liked. In fact, he was sexy as hell. Trevor identified him immediately as a working man. The jeans, boots, and T-shirt helped him peg the young man, but so did his deep tan, his close-cropped dirty blond hair, and that red bandana around his neck. It was just the sort of bandana the Stilton kid had been wearing last summer on the road crew fixing the pot holes on the road up to the Upper Head. Cole had seen Andy Stilton there, because this was where the Cole mansion was located, on the bluff to the north of the Shernhaven harbor, one of three mansions of the town founders sitting in that prominent position.

The kid—home from college for a short vacation last summer before he had to report back for football practice, Cole had known—was the flag holder for the road crew, standing at one end to hold up traffic to take its turn on the one lane they weren't working on. He'd wanted a better-paying job at the shipyard, but he couldn't be home long enough for them to hire him. That's where he was working this summer, though. There had been little traffic on the Upper Head road that day because there were only the three houses at the top of the bluff, where the road led up from its intersection with Wharf Street, at the Shern Shipyards. But Cole guessed there must have been some sort of union that made them employ flag holders regardless.

The Stilton boy wasn't home for long, so he had to take the work he could get. Cole, whether Andy knew it or not, had arranged for him to get this job. Trevor Cole prided himself in thinking ahead. The pay was OK, but it was dusty work. That was what the red bandana was for. Andy had it around his neck and would pull it up and over his mouth and nose whenever a vehicle went by and kicked up dust. The road was asphalted, but, even though it led up onto a bluff, the sand got up there on dry days like it had been last summer and kicked up a choking cloud.

Even with the bandana—especially with the bandana—Andy looked good to Cole. He liked the construction work look. It gave him a thrill to slum. And Andy was in great shape—a college football player, just like Trevor Cole himself had been at Harvard only four years previously—and had been wearing just construction boots and low-hanging shorts in addition to that bandana.

Trevor Cole didn't just know when Andy Stilton would be home from college for the summers; he also knew quite a bit about what Andy did at college.

A twenty-dollar tip to the head of the road crew and another twenty to Andy, and Andy had ridden to the top of Upper Head in Trevor's BMW convertible with him, gotten in the back seat with Cole, and let the banker suck him off before folding Trevor's belly over the tonneau cover and fucking him doggy style. The college guy had been surprised that Cole had been the one who wanted to be bottomed. He was easier to convince and handle when he'd found that out. He'd said that Cole had looked too macho to want to be the one giving it up, but Cole just laughed and said he had always been good about putting up a good façade.

Yes, Trevor Cole had fond memories of a hunk with a red bandana around his neck.

And here, standing in front of the bus station, smoking a cigarette and acting like he was considering where to strike out next, was another hunk with a red bandana around his neck. He was older than the Stilton kid was, but he looked a whole lot more experienced. It got Trevor Cole's juices flowing.

"Ben," he called out across the bank lobby. "Come over here, please."

Ben Semple, sitting at the loan officer's desk, got up and trotted over to Trevor Cole's side. Ben always answered the call of a Cole—as had his ancestors back in time.

"See that young man standing across the street?"

"Yes sir, I do."

"Want you to go over and welcome him to Shernhaven. Find out if he's new here and needs anything. Anything at all. Understand, Ben?"

11

"Yes, I do," Ben answered. And indeed he did understand. There was a very good reason he understood.

"If he needs a job or some place to stay, take care of that for him. Just say the word at the shipyard and they'll take him in. Tell them I suggested it. You can tell him it was I who set it up, too. And there's an apartment over my garage he could use for a couple of days at least."

"Yes sir, I'll tell him."

Cole watched Ben leave the bank and cross the street. His eyes went to the bulbous buttocks in the tight-fitting trousers of his loan officer. Cole loved those butt cheeks. He loved pressing his face between them just before Ben got in the mood to grab him and turn him and skewer him with that big black cock of his.

Ben Semple was another one of Cole's "slumming down" fetishes—in fact his primary one. As he watched the young black man walk away from him, like he was dancing on the balls of his feet, Cole marveled at the perfect V from massive shoulders and biceps down to a thin waist and hips and then flared buttocks bouncing along on strong thighs.

This was not your typical bank loan officer. This was more like a prize fighter or a champion bodybuilder. But the Semples had been in Shernhaven almost as long as anyone else, brought here by Trevor's own ancestors. And Trevor's ancestors went back to the beginning of the harbor town. One of the streets here was named Semple. Not a major street, though, but, to Trevor's consternation, it was almost as prominent as the street named for the Coles.

So, although Cole often made Ben put on construction boots and a bandana when they fucked—which was frequently— to the rest of the town, Ben Semple, who had been a sports hero in the minor baseball leagues before coming home, was quite acceptable. He and his family were a colorful part of the town's long history.

* * * *

"Hello, I couldn't help but notice you arrive on the bus. I don't wish to be forward, but if you're new to Shernhaven, I'd like

12

to welcome you—and help you get to where you're going if you aren't sure."

The young man looked Ben Semple over from top to bottom and gave him a little half smile that piqued the black man's interest. Cole sure can pick them, Ben thought. From across the street he could tell. He put out his hand. "Hi, my name is Ben. Ben Semple. I work in the bank across the street there. Can I help you with anything?"

The young man met Ben's hand with his and gave him a firm, assured handshake, holding on maybe a bit longer than he really needed to do. "My name's Tab. And, yes, I've come to town to try it out. How's the work around here?"

"Tab . . ."

"Just Tab. That will do. Work possibilities?"

"Sure there are possibilities. We have very low unemployment here. If you're willing to get your hands dirty—"

"Handyman or toolman or construction work. Just about anything with my hands. I'm good at fixing things."

Ben looked down at the young man's hands. They indeed looked like they'd done plenty of manual work. They were good, strong hands. Pretty much like Ben's hands would be if he hadn't wound up in an office and inside an arrangement with Trevor Cole—which he didn't much like, but which had been in his family's blood since back in the middle of the eighteenth century, when Trevor Cole's ancestor, a slave trader, had brought Ben's ancestor from Barbados.

"A handyman, eh? Plenty of work for that around here. So you've come to Shernhaven to fix us, have you?"

It was meant as an ice breaker, and it was taken that way. Tab gave Ben a wry little smile.

"You could say so, I guess. Much around here needing fixing?"

"More than it looks, maybe. Here, let's walk down along the park, and I'll help you get oriented. We have a shipyard here that's doing real well. It builds racing yachts now. And they always need good workers. It's noon. Let me treat you to a welcome lunch and then I'll walk you over to the shipyard and introduce you."

"That would be real good," Tab said, as he leaned down and picked up his duffel bag.

That had been easy, Ben thought. It was almost like the guy was on the make. Well, Ben certainly wouldn't mind making him. He looked like a real sweet piece of tail.

"We'll go to the Blue Marlin Café just over on the corner of Hobart and Cole, down closer to the wharf. That'll put us on the way to the shipyard."

Tab stiffened noticeably.

"It looks a bit like a dive, but the prices are good and so is the food," Ben said, not knowing what had caused the slight scowl on Tab's face. "It's one of the oldest buildings in town—or parts of it are. A tavern for the fisherman originally, I hear. Until recently it was a bar called Dungan's."

"That will be OK. Sounds like my kind of place."

Ben thought Tab's voice sounded rather funny, but when he looked over at the stranger in town, the young man was wearing a wary smile that looked good on him.

Over lunch, the discussion became increasingly probing and suggestive. Tab was dropping hints of his approachability, and Ben was becoming much more comfortable in alluding to his preferences as well. He also was close to forgetting that he was supposed to be setting this guy up for his boss.

"Any night life here?" Tab asked.

"Yeah, sure. Mostly out the road toward Braintree. Some motorcycle bars and girlie clubs and . . ."

"And anything else? Anywhere a guy can just . . . hang out?"

Ben laughed, a bit nervously. "If you mean just guys, there's Hernando's."

"Hernando's? That sounds pretty south of the border for Massachusetts."

Ben laughed again. "Well, yes, the Hispanics are seeping in everywhere. It was called Henry's until recently. It's over on the other side of the park at Cushing and Semple."

Tab gave him a look of surprise. "Yes, the street's named for my family. My family ran the bar there for generations—until the Hispanics started creeping in. Eventually, we just let them have it—mostly; some of my brothers still work there. But there are some really cute guys—if you like the darker skin. And if it's really guys that you like." There he'd said it about as plainly as he could.

"I like dark skinned guys just fine," Tab said, leveling his gaze at Ben.

Ben swallowed hard. The guy hadn't flinched at the "just guys" statement. He'd accepted it like it was natural. "Guess we're done here. Still want to check out the shipyard or feeling like you want to get back on the bus?"

"Oh, I don't think I want to get back on the bus today. The shipyard it is."

All it took was the invocation of Trevor Cole's name to secure a provisional handyman job for Tab at the shipyard. Ben knew from experience that the foreman of the work crew there would be quite pleased to take a guy like Tab on—in several ways, including the work angle.

"Now for some place for you to stay—unless you don't like me getting too pushy," Ben said as they were sitting at a wharf-side bar and drinking off a beer after the short interview at the shipyard, which got even shorter when Trevor Cole's name had been invoked.

"I wouldn't mind you getting pushy at all," Tab said.

"Well, Mr. Cole, my banker boss, says he has a small empty apartment over his garage you could stay in for a while. He lives up there in the big house on what we call the Upper Head—on the bluff above the shipyard. You could—"

"Where do you live?"

Ben hesitated. A chill went up his spine. Why was this so easy?

"Right here on the wharf—my apartment is in the building over there, with a good view out over the marina of the boat basin. I've got a great view of the fishing boats going out in the morning as I do my workout."

"Interested in proving it to me?"

"What?"

"That the view's good. And that you can give a guy a good workout."

15

They fucked on an exercise mat in front of the French doors that opened out onto a third-floor balcony from which, in their position, all they saw were the tops of masts of sailboats docked at the yacht club below.

The exercise mat was the appropriate equipment for them, because there was the initial wrestle for who was going to fuck whom. In the end they both got their turn.

Neither had been quite so picky about exchanging cock sucks. While Ben was in the kitchenette breaking a couple of beers out of the refrigerator, Tab stripped down to his briefs and was waiting on the sofa. When Ben returned, there were no romantic preliminaries. As soon as he sat down next to Tab, Tab reached over and unzipped him. He pulled out Ben's cock, said he was pleased to see both that it was already half hard and that it was worth the trip, and immediately deep-throated him and began going down on him in a steady rhythm.

Ben managed to strip off his clothes as he groaned and moaned in the pleasure of a more soft and expert mouth than Trevor Cole had. It was Ben who moved them to a 69 position on the sofa and began going down on Tab as well.

He murmured something Tab didn't hear when Tab moved out of that stance, pushed Ben up to a seated position, and knelt on the carpet between his legs, lifting the young black man's beefy thighs over his shoulders. Tab's tongue went down Ben's taint, that strip of flesh between the base of the balls and the asshole, and into the crack between his butt cheeks and explored, eventually with the help of his fingers.

Ben laid back and moaned at first, his hands massaging Tab's scalp, but then he started to get the idea of what Tab was moving toward. Ben muttered an objection and started to push Tab's head away from between his butt cheeks. Tab licked back to where he had started, swallowed Ben's cock, and started to work it.

"Hey, we'd better . . . I'm gonna come if we . . ." But it was too late, because Ben did come then in Tab's mouth. This was when they first kissed, with Tab rising on his knees and pulling Ben's head down to his and giving him a deep kiss on the mouth, lubricated by Ben's cum.

Ben, the stronger of the two, lifted Tab up and sat him on the sofa next to him, and this time it was he who went down between Tab's knees and resumed his sucking of Tab's cock.

Before he could make Tab come, though, the young white man pulled away and stood. He fisted Ben's wrist and pulled him up off the sofa with a laugh, guided him over to the exercise mat in front of the French doors, pushed him down, and landed on top of him.

Sitting up, he said, "You got any?"

"Rubbers?"

"Yeah."

When Ben returned from the bedroom, he had already rolled one on himself, clearly signaling who he thought was going to be fucked.

"That was supposed to be for me. So, you like it bareback?" Tab growled. "That's OK with me."

He grabbed Ben's ankle and pulled him off balance. The two were flattened in a heap and the wrestling match had begun. It was a good match, but Ben was the stronger of the two. He got Tab onto his belly, with Ben stretched on his back and getting him in a full Nelson.

Ben leaned his mouth into Tab's ear and whispered. "Tell me you've been fucked before."

"Yeah, I've been fucked before, but . . . oh shit!"

Tab was being fucked again. And Ben was as hard as a rock. He'd recovered nicely from the blow job on the sofa. He proceeded to show just how good a shape he was in, while Tab groaned at the deep-seated entry. He squirmed and moaned and encouraged Ben for deeper and more vigorous penetration, and Ben held him in thrall with a choke hold and his sword pinning Tab to the mat.

"You . . . really do a good workout," Tab said with a groan when he could manage to talk at all.

"And you've proven yourself as a handyman," Ben answered.

Tab pulled himself from under Ben and sat up on the mat beside him, taking his head in both of his hands and pulling Ben's face to his and into a deep kiss.

Ben didn't even feel the pressure of Tab's fingers on the tender points on his neck until his head was swimming from the lack of oxygen. About the time he learned he was under attack, he blacked out and keeled over onto the mat.

When Ben came to—and not fully then for several minutes—it was too late to defend the virginity of his channel. He was on his back on the mat, with Tab kneeling between his thighs, his knees up under Ben's buttocks, and Tab was already fucking him in long, deep strokes.

Ben was hurting, but it was a hurt that was swamped with a feeling of pleasure and utter taking that he had never known was possible. He began to resist, but he felt Tab's fingers starting to dig at the arteries in his neck again and to become woozy.

"We'll both enjoy it more if you are awake for it," Tab said in a low voice. "You're great at wrestling, but I've taken an Oriental martial arts class or two. I let you fuck me when you won at wrestling; only fair to let me fuck you when I've won."

Ben's answer was a long moan.

"Going to stay awake? Good." Tab loosened his grip on Ben's neck but kept his hands there, ready to take charge again. "Better when you are awake for it. You've got a sweet, tight ass. And don't worry, I found the rubbers in your bedroom."

Ben indeed was enjoying it now. He encircled Tab with his arms and stroked his shoulder blades with his fingers in the rhythm of the fuck. He hooked his heels on Tab's thighs and rubbed them up in down in cadence as well. Even his hips were moving with Tab. And when Tab came with a little cry, so did Ben.

When they were able to speak again, they were laying in each other's arms, their legs entwined, both of them looking through the panes of glass in the French doors to the masts of the sailing vessels below.

"Sorry, but I like it both ways," Tab murmured. "I think you take it both ways too, don't you?"

"Yeah. Sometimes."

"These welts on your back, buttocks, and thighs. Did Cole do this? Is that what he's like?"

"No. Not Cole. He's not the only one with the power around here to get guys like me to do the dirty with them—and in ways they like. Shernhaven is that sort of town. Maybe you need to understand that before you decide to stay here for any length of time."

Tab gave Ben time to say more about that, but when he didn't, he changed the subject. "It was a good fuck. One of the best. So, do we go look at this Cole guy's garage apartment or . . . ?"

"Or you can stay here if you want."

"In your apartment, with you?"

"In my bed, with me."

"Will your boss, Cole, like that? I got the impression he was having you set me up for him."

"He was. No, he wouldn't like it . . . if he knew you were staying here. And not just because he wouldn't be getting a crack at you. Because I fuck him, and although he doesn't accept any 'one and only' responsibility, he expects me to."

"So, it might be difficult?"

"Fuck it. I want you to stay. You get settled here. I've got to go back to the office."

Tab laid there on the exercise mat, recovering from the workout, as Ben went to the shower and then redressed and left the apartment.

"Here's a set of keys in case you go out," he said, throwing them across the room to Tab as he left.

Tab waited until he was sure Ben was gone and then he got up from the mat and padded around the apartment, looking into this and that, being careful to return everything to where he found it. He wasn't looking for anything in particular, but there was no telling what he might find that would help him.

Then he went in and took a shower. He came back into the living room with a towel around his waist and sat down on the sofa and reached for the beer he hadn't gotten to drink before the fun and games started. He laid back into the sofa, put his feet up on the coffee table, looked up at the ceiling, and smiled.

This had been easier than he'd supposed it would be. He hadn't planned to start with Semple and Cole, but he had certainly planned to get around to sticking it to Trevor Cole. Now to see what he could do to move Ben out of Cole's bed and ass more permanently and into bed with him instead—along with all of the rest he had to do here in Shernhaven.

"Here's to you, Dad," he called out to the empty room, as he lifted his beer bottle in a salute.

Chapter One: 1640

The gentlemen, the three principles of the expedition, Peter Cushing, Daniel Hobart, and Addis Shern, were conversing at the rail when Captain Lynch sidled up to them from out of the darkness. He always felt so inferior—and, he thought, was treated as such—when he approached their counsel. But he was the captain of this vessel, not any one of the three of them, and that meant something, even if they did not act as if they countenanced it. They were not in command until they reached land. Out here on the sea he was in command.

The men grew silent as he approached, and Lynch heard a seaman sing out from the rigging a melodious "Land ho." He'd been doing so periodically all evening and into the night more as a warning that they may be moving into shallow waters than as a first sighting of terra firma after the forty-eight days they'd been on the waters from England to this new world.

They had first landed at Plymouth, to the south, and were now sailing north, working on identifying and putting in at the land grant Charles I had given to the lords Cushing, Hobart, and Shern.

That must be the young sailor, Thomas Cole, singing from the mainmast, Lynch thought. And he couldn't keep himself from licking his lips in arousal. Nice fresh piece that, he thought. He'd intended to get to that on this voyage—and sooner than now, when they were close to their destination. Clear tenor singing voice. Almost angelic. It would be—no, will be—a pleasure, he thought. He couldn't think of any better pastime than debauching angels.

As the three principals came to realize that Lynch was not going to leave his position at their elbows—and decorum required that they not snub him noticeably, at least in the presence of the deck crew—they picked up their conversation again, albeit an entirely different discussion than the one they had been conducting. Now it was focused on the cry of land that they'd heard from the rigging. All three leaned forward and looked intensely into the dusk as the form of twin bluffs, one of which was a curved spit out into the ocean, began to take shape to port of the vessel as it cut through the waves headed north along the North American continent.

"That may be it," said Shern.

"Yea, it is described as that appears," agreed Hobart. "A natural harbor, nearly circular, abutted by two sharp-cliffed headlands, one of which is likened to an arm curving out into the ocean. That do look like our land grant."

"And not too soon," chimed in Cushing. "It be positioned between Plymouth to the south and Boston to the north and we left Plymouth not long after sunrise. I afear that if this be it not, we have overshot and will be in Boston by tomorrow's dawn."

"Captain," Hobart said, turning toward the hunch-backed, rat-faced Irishman nosing in at their elbows at the rails. "Heave to here, if you please. In the morning's light we'll send out a party to determine if this be our destination." He was doing what he could to hold back his distaste for the ship's captain, who looked the part of a highwayman and who he and his fellow noblemen highly suspected of unclean and un-Christian practices.

"As you please, M'Lord," Captain Lynch said in a deferential manner, lowering his eyes and bowing slightly. He would be pleased if this were the proper spot and he could be rid of these fopperies forthwith. But his mind wasn't on them. If this was the spot and they all made land, he no longer would be in command—at least until he could get back to his ship.

This meant that the intentions he'd long had for the seaman Cole should be brought to fruition tonight, for he had heard Addis Shern sweet talking the lad and was afraid he would pirate Cole away to the land once they had arrived. Lynch wanted the first taking, the deflowering, to be highly entertaining—and to be his to enjoy. He thought Shern would lose interest once Cole was debauched by another, and then he himself could savor the conquest with follow-on fuckings of the lad on the sail back to England.

Calling out to the master of the watch, the captain set into motion the anchoring of the ship. Then he called up into the rigging, "You, sailor Thomas Cole. Shinny down here and fetch a bottle of rum from the stores and bring it to my cabin."

Then, with almost a celebratory leer of having outfoxed them at the three land grant gentlemen at the rails, which made all three of them wince, he turned and strode to his cabin.

Although technically innocent—at least of the ultimate sin—the young, blond sailor, Thomas Cole, was not stupid. As he was descending slowly from the rigging, much more slowly than if it had been a rations call, his mind was racing. He had known other young sailors who were told to deliver rum to the captain's quarters and who came back to the forecastle bowlegged, sniveling, and half out of their minds. And he had known he had had the captain's eye for most of the voyage already.

He was afraid. Not so much afraid of the act, which he had seen and heard the sailors performing with each other in the darkness of the night in the far corners of the forecastle, but more of the captain, who was a cruel and gnarled monster. In whisperings when other sailors had come back from the captain's cabin and sat alone and unresponding in the shadows, rocking back and forth and whimpering until the necessities of life before the mast enveloped them once more in the daily chores and challenges of a sailor, he had heard tales of the captain and of his cruelty. But mostly, he had heard tails of a cock that could split a man in two.

This brought fear into young Thomas Cole's mind. But it brought arousal and curiosity, as well.

Thomas had always been too curious for his own good— and too angelic of face and willowy of body. Back in his village in Dorset, although he had done nothing to earn the reputation, he came to be known as a tease to a certain type of older man. These rumors had reached the ears of his parents, who, in consternation, had seen him shipped off to sea—as much to save the family reputation as to protect his virtue.

His first voyage was this one, on the ship captained by Mortimer Lynch.

Truth be known, Thomas hadn't minded the attentions of the older men of his village—the tentative touchings and special attentions in the rectory by the cleric of his church had been particularly interesting to him. But there was nothing definite that Thomas could identify as being the reason. Just being himself—an angelic-looking, lithe-figured young man with a mop of golden hair and fair of face—seemed to be all that would explain why he had to be so secretly and quickly whisked to the nearest seaport.

He had begun to understand what it was all about when he was warned upon embarking on Lynch's ship to pick a hammock near the door into the forecastle, which was, he was told, perhaps the least private and noisiest spot, but also the safest for him.

It wasn't long before he learned why, as the noises of the night in the forecastle slowly informed him of happenings in the shadowy corners—and the types of low guttural moans and sighs that were mildly similar to what he remembered hearing in the rectory when the cleric was helping him put on his alb before services.

There was another young man on the voyage, though, who had caught young Cole's interest. Edward Geer. He wasn't a sailor. A brawny, dark-haired, hirsute young man with brooding good looks, Geer was a carpenter's apprentice in the entourage of the gentleman, Peter Cushing. He didn't bunk in the forecastle, which was reserved for the ship's sailors. But there were other, remote, dark places in the ship. Places where, after Thomas and Edward had taken up a friendship in bantering and shared mirth on the deck, the two could repair to more quiet—and, eventually, more intimate discussions.

The ship was no more than a week out of Weymouth before Edward and Thomas were exploring each other's bodies with trembling hands, eventually each, while lips found lips, finding the other's cock with their hands and providing mutual relief—and, somewhat to their surprise, mutual pleasure.

Thomas might have gone farther with Edward, but a week out of Plymouth Landing in the New World, he was taken with affright at the danger that might be putting Edward in. The longer the voyage, the randier the sailors got—and the braver and more demanding.

A bruiser of a muscle man they all called the Greek and who, rumor had it, was determined to debauch his way through all of the "taker" sailors ere the ship reached land, grabbed Thomas from his hammock one night and was forcibly carrying him to the rear of the forecastle, telling a trembling Thomas in no uncertain terms what he was going to do with him. But before the Greek could carry through with his plan, the coxswain, summoned by another sailor, had come down into the forecastle with a belaying pin in his hand and commanded that the Greek not manhandle Thomas, with the statement, "Captain Lynch has declared this one not be touched."

The effect on the Greek was frightening in and of itself. He immediately let Thomas slip to the floor and slunk away.

Thomas thanked the coxswain, only to be told that there was no real thanks to be giving—that the captain was making such a declaration because he intended to have Thomas himself. From the look that accompanied this declaration, Thomas understood that he was being pitied—but more than that, that the coxswain was trying to save his own ass.

"Ye still be a virgin to the cock of man, be ye not?" the coxswain had bluntly asked.

"Yes," Thomas answered, being truthfully able to answer that, as his fondlings with Edward had not yet gone that far—if he caught the coxswain's meaning well enough—even though he had hopes of it.

"Then keep it that way. I have put the word out. If another man takes what the captain wants from you, you must tell me. The captain should not find this out for his own. It would be worth the hide of all of us. And, for that man's sake, give him fair warning of the captain's privilege before he do touch you—if you have any mercy in you. Because if he do touch you, he is a dead man."

It was after this scene in the forecastle that Thomas paid increased attention to the sailors staggering back from their rum delivery to the captain's quarters and whisperings were made to him of the captain's cruelty and the fearsomeness of his manhood.

Upon arrival in Plymouth Landing, when Edward Geer sought Thomas out to go to an aft storage locker with him, sighing of his need for Thomas before they must be parted, Thomas told him that he could not. He said that Geer would be arriving at his own destination on land soon and Thomas would be sailing away with the ship—and that he had enjoyed his private moments with Geer, but that it should get no more serious than it had. What he didn't tell Edward was that he was afraid of what the captain would do to both of them if he heard they were being intimate.

Geer was hurt and avoided Thomas for the rest of the journey. But there wasn't much Thomas could do about that but mark his own regret.

It was thus that, on the night before the landing upon the shores of what was, indeed, the land grant given to Hobart, Cushing, and Shern, Thomas Cole had few illusions about what it meant for the captain to summon him to his quarters with a flagon of rum.

As Thomas entered the captain's dimly lit cabin, illuminated only by a few candles in sconces upon the walls and the small panes of glass at the stern of the ship looking out into the starry night, he arrived as any other sailor on the vessel would—burned bronze by the sun, hard bodied, bare-chested, and barefooted and with only straight-legged, once-white cotton breeches held up with a rope belt. He was far from the angelic boy who embarked on the journey, looking far younger than his calendar years. He was now a beautiful, curly golden-haired young man of ripe body.

Thomas found the captain sitting behind a wooden desk facing the door. He was writing something on paper with a quill pen and continued to do so, head down, for several minutes after Thomas entered the room. The scratching of the quill was only heightening Thomas's apprehension.

"Place the flagon on the desk and step back." Captain Lynch didn't look up.

Thomas did as was he was bidden and escaped to stand near the door, which he'd left open, hoping he would be permitted to withdraw.

"Shut the door and come closer into the light."

Thomas complied.

"Unknot the rope at your waist and hand it to me."

"But then my—"

"Yes, they will. Do you question my orders young man?"

"No, no sir," Thomas answered in a stumble. His trembling hands went to the knot at his waist, and he struggled to loosen the rope. When he'd accomplished that, Thomas was only able to hold his trousers up by grabbing the waistband with his hands.

"Take your hands away."

With a sigh of the inevitable, Thomas did so, and his trousers fell to the floor. He stood naked in the flickering light, he moved his hands to cover his manhood, but a low growl from Lynch stopped him in mid swing.

"Leave your hands at your side."

Captain Lynch then looked up and gave Thomas a hard gaze.

"This is your first sea voyage, is it not, Sailor Cole?"

"Aye, sir. Aye, Captain, it is."

"But ye know of the law of the sea, don't ye?"

"Aye. Yes sir."

"Ye know that on a vessel on the water, the captain is king?"

"Aye, sir."

"And that all on board serve at the captain's pleasure."

"Aye, sir." This time not so smartly answered.

"And, more important, to serve the captain's pleasure."

Thomas didn't answer; he just let his head tip forward and his eyes raced over the worn boards at his bare feet, as if some escape hatch would magically appear. But the captain didn't really require an answer. He was just enjoying the affirmation of his power at sea. "Even to a judgment of death if the captain be not pleased?"

"Aye, sir."

"Ye have heard, no doubt, of what pleases this captain."

Thomas couldn't bring himself to answer this.

"Do ye?"

27

"Aye, sir," Thomas managed to voice in a low tone.

"Ye will pleasure me."

It wasn't a question. Again, it prompted a somewhat reluctant, "Aye, sir."

"Good, then." Captain Lynch dropped the quill on the paper and stood up from the desk.

Thomas gasped. Lynch was wearing nothing below his jacket, and his cock was monstrously prepared for sport.

He walked around the desk, circled Thomas twice, and stopped behind him—very close behind him. Thomas could feel the man's hot breath on his neck. Then he felt the palm of a hand at his waist, which moved around and up his heaving belly to his chest. Thomas gasped as a nipple was tweaked. Edward had never done this to him. But thinking back, he vaguely remembered the cleric having touched him there in the village in Dorset.

The captain's other hand went to Thomas's quivering butt cheeks, and Thomas jerked and gave a little surprised grunt as a thick finger breached his channel hole.

Edward had done this—although only this, not going any farther. And Thomas was suddenly worried that Edward had gone too far. That this was enough for Thomas not to be able to claim to be a virgin.

The hand on his chest moved down his belly, cupped his balls briefly, and then grasped his cock hard. Thomas gasped again, and his whole body began to shake. The captain laughed a low laugh. .

"Ye do respond as a virgin," the captain murmured. Thomas was flooded with gratitude that the captain would think that, and his body relaxed.

"Yes, it's best that ye do lose the tension," the captain said. "It will go much better for ye if ye are not tight in ways that tightness does not please me. Aye, ye can tighten on that. And draw it in. Aye, like that. Ye declare that ye be virgin to a man's cock inside you?"

"Aye," Thomas whispered.

Thomas sphincter muscle had capitulated to the pressing of Lynch's finger, and the captain had deepened his penetration of the channel—helped, as he said, by a natural response of the

28

channel now to draw the finger in. Thomas was surprised and gasped and tightened up briefly again as a second finger was inserted.

The captain was sucking on Thomas's neck and working Thomas's cock with fast, long strokes of his fist.

Edward had stroked him off more slowly and with less pressure. Thomas came with a little cry. His knees tried to buckle, but the captain's hand left his cock and palmed Thomas's belly to hold him in place.

The captain had three fingers in Thomas's ass channel—deep—and Thomas moaned and felt his channel slackening.

"Ye want me now, don't ye?"

Thomas didn't answer.

"Don't ye?"

"Aye," he whispered, and, in fact, he did want it now. That he wanted it from Edward rather than this old, grotesque monster was beside the point.

"Aye, who? And I don't mean captain. I mean to be acknowledged as much more."

"Aye . . . Master," Thomas whispered. And he must have guessed right, as the captain laughed at the hearing of his control being acknowledged.

The captain lifted Thomas up with an arm around his waist, swiveled him toward the stern, and slammed him down on the desk on his belly.

Thomas's sensations were the loss of breath at the sudden, brutal movement and the feel of the quill shaft and feather on his sternum, both of which were overwhelmed immediately by a scream—his—and the searing pain of his ass channel being penetrated and stretched to the limit.

Purchase inside Thomas having been achieved, the captain pinned Thomas to the desk top with his chest, reached out and grabbed Thomas's wrists with his fists. He held Thomas's arms out wide and latched onto the skin between the young man's shoulder blades with his teeth. He pulled Thomas's arms together again and used the young man's own rope belt to tie his wrists together and to an iron ring over the edge of the far side of the desk.

Then, as Thomas wailed his pain and violation in tones that eventually subsided into gurgles of surrender and moans of the advent of pleasure and acceptance, Captain Lynch pounded his ass hard and deep.

After the captain had come, he untied the semiconscious Thomas, lifted his body up as if Thomas was of no weight at all, and pushed him down on his knees. Turning his body to him and perching on the desk, the captain took Thomas's head in both hands, moved Thomas's face to his dripping cock, and said. "Clean it."

After doing so, Thomas learned the rudiments of cock sucking, gagging and sobbing all the way.

When the captain was hard again, he picked Thomas up and slammed him down hard on the desktop on his back and slapped his legs wide.

"Please," Thomas pleaded. "Yes, again. But, please. Can we do it on your bed? And in the dark?"

The captain laughed, but he complied. And he soon found out that Thomas was a quick study in learning how to please a man, not knowing that Thomas could take it much better without seeing the captain's ugly countenance.

Thomas stumbled back to the forecastle, bowlegged, and sobbing, and staggering as much as any before him had. But unlike most before him, possibly all, Thomas came back with the revelation that, as long as it was done in the dark, he loved having the captain's cock working inside him—and determined that he would have as much of that, from as many a well-hung man as possible—as he could get.

* * * *

"This would be a natural place for the repair of our ships. The channel is deep right near here. We can easily dredge the rest of the distance."

Cushing, Hobart, and Shern were standing on the short beach at the north of the natural harbor. Hobart, who had spoken, was holding charts and already planning in his mind where construction would begin. Cushing was calculating the actual

30

construction needs for the first of the buildings they would need. Shern was lost in the dream of the boatyard he would found in this spot. That purpose had already been conceded to him within the wording of the king's land grant.

"Hobart will be a fitting name for this place. The siting is almost ideal. The harbor will be both snug and safe. The wharves will go at the other end of the curve there. We can call the bluff above this boatyard location the Upper Headland. And that curve of cliff running around the spit to the south end of the harbor the Lower Headland."

Ye can give the names as you please, Daniel Hobart, Shern thought for now. That were a privilege granted ye by King Charles. But we shall see what we shall see. And I do rightly know that my own dwelling will be built at the top of what ye named the Upper Headland. Overlooking the boatyard and whatever town we build. And it will be built higher on the headland ere yours ever will be.

What he said aloud, though, was, "The town will need a common. We must mark it as English."

"Yes, yes," Hobart answered, almost with irritation at anyone else but him plotting the town. "First, though, we must blaze paths to Boston in the north and Braintree to the west. We must establish our links with the other settlements and begin providing for the goods we need—both for ourselves and with Mother England."

"Yes, we've discussed the need for more help once we've put down roots here," Cushing said. "We must ship back to England almost immediately. With Captain Lynch, regrettably. I do not like the idea of a return sea voyage with him, but if we let him go, there is no telling when the next ship will be able to take us."

"Yes," Hobart said, almost absently, already looking out over the land rise from the harbor for the best placement of the common ground Shern had mentioned. "But one of us will need to stay. The town will not build itself."

"Yes, one of use will need to stay," Shern answered. He smiled grimly to himself, determined who that one would be.

31

Cushing bustled off then to attend to the longboats arriving from the ship with the last porting of the supplies to help get the town started.

Captain Lynch and his coxswain were overseeing this operation as well as the unpacking of the tents. They would stay on land too, until all of the provisions were stored where they needed to be and the tent city was erected.

The carpenter, young Edward Geer, was leading a group of men into the fringe of trees to the west of the town plot. He would identify trees for felling, and they would start construction of wooden buildings almost immediately.

In his group, at the behest of Addis Shern, was another young carpenter who was secretly tasked to look only for trees appropriate for building boats. Shern was fully determined to make the boatyard the first—and premier—economic enterprise of the new town.

Out beyond the mouth of the harbor lay the ship languidly at anchor. A crew of ten had been left on board to ensure that the ship could be safely sailed should an expected squall arise. The Greek was left in charge of the crew. Young Thomas Cole was one of the sailors on the ship, because the ship's captain could not risk having him on land under the authority of Addis Shern. Neither Captain Lynch nor the coxswain would be back on board for at least a day.

There was little to do as long as the ship was resting peacefully at anchor.

Thomas Cole wasn't angry about what the captain did to him the previous night. He had been expecting it, and, in various ways he had been building up to it. What was unexpected was how much he had enjoyed having a man's cock working inside him—to have that much control of another man's desires and to be desired by another man so much that the man lost total control in his lust. Being with the captain in the dark enabled Cole to concentrate on his cock and his ability to use it. The ugliness of him melted away in the dark. And having tasted what a man could receive from another man, Thomas was itching for a repeat helping of it.

The Greek was snoozing, naked, in his hammock. He was having a wet dream, and Thomas became mesmerized at watching the brute of a man's cock harden and the sailor's hand go to it and work it even though he was asleep. The man awoke to the sensation of Thomas practicing what the captain had taught him the night before in cock sucking.

With a bellow and a heave of Thomas's body over his, Thomas was skewered and was dancing his ass on the Greek's staff. The Greek wasn't as large as the captain but he was more vigorous, and Thomas's endurance was pushed to the edge of glorious endurance as, the Greek gripping his waist between two rough, calloused hands, he was slammed up and down hard time and again on that thick rod until he was flooded in the Greek's victory.

The other eight men gathered around, fascinated and aroused. And when the Greek finished, Thomas took on anyone else who wanted him for the price of two coppers. After all eight of the others were exhausted, Thomas had twenty coppers he'd never had before.

It was almost too easy, especially since he had enjoyed himself.

The captain and coxswain didn't return to the ship for three days, and Thomas was suddenly one of the richest men between Boston and Plymouth.

Longboats did, however, go back and forth between the ship and land, and on the evening of the third day, a sailor who had been to the quickly rising town that day took Thomas aside and told him that one of the other sailors had informed the captain what Thomas was doing and that he could surely expect a flogging or worse when the captain was back on board.

That night, tying his new fortune in a canvas bag around his neck, Thomas slipped into the water and swam to the Lower Headland spit. When he reached the town, he sought out Edward Geer, who had already built a lean-to shed opening to the back of his tent.

Edward was on his back on a pallet, naked, and sleeping the sleep of a man who had put in a hard day's work. Thomas stretched out beside him, took Edward's lips in his, and moved a

33

hand down his body to encase the young carpenter's cock. Edward moaned and came to life as Thomas's mouth followed the path his hand had opened up, ending by closing his lips over Edward's now-erect cock.

Edward came then. And later he came as Thomas rode his hips with his pelvis. And then again before dawn when Edward asserted himself and pushed Thomas's back down on the pallet, spread Thomas's legs, and fucked his new-found lover hard and deep.

The next morning Thomas showed Edward the bag full of coppers, informed him how they had been acquired, and told him of his plan for establishing both of them in this New World and new town.

Edward was not pleased at first, but when Thomas said the other alternative was for Thomas to return to the ship and fuck the captain all the way back to England. Edward liked that plan even less and didn't question Thomas more. Thomas, of course, had no intention of following such a plan as that at all. He knew that once he and the captain were back on the ship together on the high seas, he would be completely at the captain's whim, and that it very likely would not go well for him at all.

Thomas was also aware that there was another alternative for him now that he was on land. Addis Shern had already made advances and offers. If Thomas could not lie under Edward, he surely could do that for Addis Shern. Although Shern was a figure of higher authority, though, Thomas did not prefer him, as he had heard that Shern had a mean streak in his taking that included a whip.

But there was no particular reason for Edward to know either that the threat to return to the captain was a ruse or that Thomas had a backup plan with Addis Shern. Edward was a big, arousing bear with a fine fucking technique. But he certainly wasn't the brighter of the two.

Edward hid Thomas in his tent and lean-to, which in the next few days he added to as he could to make it serve Thomas's plans, until Captain Lynch returned to his ship—along with Peter Cushing and Daniel Hobart—and the ship had sailed. Lynch had too much on his mind to think of his sailor, Thomas Cole, until his ship had sailed too far from the coast to return for the simple pleasure of punishing a young tease like Thomas.

Edward Geer was left in charge of the construction of the town, which gave him status and certain privileges. One of the first establishments he finished off—rising out of the tent and lean-to he himself had first occupied—served not only as his home but also as a male brothel. This business at first was "manned" by Thomas Cole only, but later, when it became established as a tavern, it employed other willing men and, when women started to arrive, them as well.

But for the first settlers, all men, Hobart having died on the voyage home followed by Cushing on the voyage back, arrived with new settlers and more provisions, there were only men. Men had to be serviced. And when there were only other men available for that, most men made do—and eventually grew to enjoy it.

It wasn't long before Thomas Cole and Edward Geer were almost as rich as the owner of the boatyard, one of the original land grantees, Addis Shern. Almost. This "almost" could be clearly seen from the town. To the south of the town, on the bluff overlooking the harbor that Hobart had named the Upper Headland, was—at the very apex, the expanding mansion of Addis Shern. A bit lower on the bluff, to the west of the Shern house, was the Cole house. To the west and a bit lower than that was the Geer house. These three families owned the entire top of the bluff. From this time forward, those living in these houses were recognized as the preeminent citizens of the town.

Before the resupply ship returned to the New World, too, there had been a change in the name of the new town. It was now named Shernhaven. Addis Shern had known the advantage of being the one to stay behind. Cushing and Hobart weren't forgotten, though. The street curving around the harbor at the water's edge was named Wharf Street, but the one parallel to that, inland, from Wharf Street, was Hobart Street. This connected at its south end to the Lower Head Road, leading out to the end of the Lower Head spit and on its north end to the Boston Road. The next parallel street to Hobart, with the commons running between them on Main Street, was Cushing Street.

Chapter Two: 1740–50

Crashing through the undergrowth of the tropical trees in the hot, humid air, Kweku fought to understand where he'd gone wrong. It wasn't his fault that Nana Opuku Ware, the Ashanti King, favored him, a by-blow, over the son who would be king, Okyere.

Kweku had overheard Okyere whining to the king, telling him that Kweku was revealing to the Dutch team camped out on the river bank the locations of the locations of the gold digs the Ashanti had concealed between the Ankobra and Volta rivers.

But he hadn't done that. He had been in the forest the whole time, clearing timber. He hadn't talked to the outlanders; not to any of them. It had been Okyere that Kweku had seen conversing with those others—the English. Kweku honored his king and supported his people's teasing of the Europeans with the yellow grit they so wanted to take away from Ashanti.

Had Okyere found out that Kweku had seen him with the snatchers of men?

Or was this all because Okyere was jealous. This is what Kweku believed. Okyere was jealous of the favor the king bestowed on Kweku, even though Kweku had no intention of challenging Okyere when the time of the kings came. Kweku had always been careful to be friendly and deferential with Okyere and to remain on his sunny side—not that Okyere had a sunny side. Kweku's mother had taught him that he had to do that to survive. Kweku would never forget what his mother had drummed into him.

But it didn't matter what Kweku did. It only mattered that Okyere saw the threat and saw the favor the king showed to Kweku.

Kweku could hear the beaters off to his left. If he could make it to the river, he could swim across and they would not know where he had gone. He could send a message to his father—the man he could not call father but who treated him as a son. He could send a message and all would be well. He would say nothing of Okyere and his jealous ways and his lying ways. No, even now Kweku could not say such a thing about Okyere in his father's ear. That would get Okyere exactly what he wanted; that would be playing into Okyere's designs. Kweku was not looking for a fight. Kweku was a man of peace. He knew that there were those who could not believe this because of his warrior stature and his strength. And yes, the beauty and fullness of his body. The men of the village hid their women from him, even now, when Kweku was barely beyond the manhood ritual.

The river. The beaters were coming close. He had to make it to the river. Turn right down this path and . . . Humphh!

Kweku looked down from the netting that held him prisoner in the trees above the path.

He was not alone. He should have guessed. Okyere stood below him, grinning up at him. Kweku's heart sank as he saw that Okyere was not alone. Beside him stood two of the English. The men Kweku had seen Okyere talking to before. Those men who came up the river in empty boats—and returned with filled boats. The men came, and after they left, the village was missing a few men, women, and even children.

Kweku did not have to guess what Okyere was up to. Why he was standing there, smiling, beside the two English. A dead Kweku might be a found Kweku and might lead to questions Okyere would not wish to have to stand before King Nana Opuku Ware and answer.

A Kweku seen walking in chains between two English to their boat on the water and then never seen again was a missing Kweku that the king of the Ashanti all too well could understand.

* * * *

Kweku did not see the light of day for longer than he could count. He could not, of course, count time. Kweku needed

37

the change from light to dark and back to dark to be able to count the passage of time. And since all was dark and dank and putrid in the belly of this vast vessel wallowing on the endless sea, it did not matter whether he could count.

Time meant little to him now. He had been betrayed. And he knew, because it was that way with the others led off to the river in chains between two English, that he would not be going back to the kingdom of the Ashanti again—at least not any time soon. And, of course, time had no real meaning for him now.

He could not blame Okyere, though. Kweku was man enough to know that if he was the one who was the king's son and Okyere the bastard, he, Kweku, would have done the same. Or perhaps not. Perhaps he would have been at least honorable enough just to kill Okyere and not to make him suffer for a birth and a favoring that were not his choice. But there was nothing to be gained to think about it further. Kweku lived in a new world now—for as long as he lived.

Only survival had meaning. Finding food and water, even moving in this mass of chained and moaning humanity in the darkness of the belly of the vessel was all he thought of. And increasingly he didn't think of that either—and as interminable time of misery oozed on, even survival was not something he cared much of.

If he could not live Ashanti—clean and standing tall under the trees of his forests—why live at all? Others around him, here in the stinking darkness of the vessel, had already made that decision. Perhaps they were the brave, pure ones. Perhaps his was the shame for clinging to a life that no longer was Ashanti.

But just about the time he was ready to fight his instincts and give his life up, he could smell a change on the breeze, even here in the fetid belly of the vessel. He could smell the scent of land and plants. And he lurched against the man shackled to him, dead for endless time already, giving off a smell that Kweku had already adjusted to—because he had no other choice—as the vessel banged up against something hard.

He was soon to learn that they had arrived on the Caribbean island of Barbados, on the other side of the great sea from Kweku's own land. And he found that the wooden dock they had banged up against ran onto the land, upon which stood many tall dwellings. Some of these structures were built of wood and others were constructed of stone and smooth, hard mud and were taller and far more numerous than the squat thatch and mud homes his own village was made of. And there were English for as far as he could see—walking purposely and gathering in groups. All looking busy but not being busy doing much of anything. All stinking of English in their choking layers of cloth under the hot sun. The ones Kweku saw who were doing anything, usually at great exertion and who did not stink because they knew what not to put on their bodies, were like him—black. From Africa. Some were Ashanti, like him. A few even looked like Ashanti he had known. But they weren't anything like they had been when he had known them. In their own village they had stood tall and walked proudly—even when bearing burdens. Here they were bent over, seeing nothing but the ground or the booted feet of the stinking English.

Kweku could barely walk as he was led in chains onto the dock—freed now of the truly dead weight of the man who had keened for endless time of his lost loved ones, until his keening had grown dim and eventually had stopped altogether.

The sun was too bright for Kweku, after all of the darkness, and he stumbled and received, with shock, the splashing of the water on his naked body from a bucket, with no preparation that it was happening. Still, he would have welcomed a second dousing. And a mouthful or two of the cool water as well.

"This one is the sturdiest. He should take the best price."

"I agree. Look at the musculature. And see the manhood and balls on the darkie. He would be good in your fields—and even better in the beds of your black females, wouldn't he, Nathan? You have always said you wanted more of them. You could have a new one in each season from each of your females if you put this one to work."

Kweku's eyesight was beginning to clear now. They had been shoved, staggering—the survivors of the journey—straight to a platform near where the dock met the land. There, while Kweku tried to focus on the hated wooden vessel that had taken

39

him away from his home to who knows where, he was sold to Nathan Semple of Semple Hill.

"Take him to the wagon, Jim and Joshia. Leave him in chains. He doesn't look like he has fight in him, but he be a real stud of a darkie. I would not want him to escape or, more likely, be stolen from me by one of my neighbors. We shall see what we shall see in how long it takes to train him to the fields and how easily he can handle that and provide me new stock as well. I be going to the tavern for a snort. Put him in the wagon. We will let him ride part way to Semple Hill. He do look all in."

Kweku understood none of this, of course. But he was a bright man—and a survivor. Soon he would understand well enough. For now, he laid back on sacking on the floor of the wagon and hoped that wherever the English had gone, he would be there for a long time. Smelling the salt sea air and watching the branches of the trees wave above his head was glorious and took him right into sleep. Almost into sleep. The two the English had sent him off in chains with were dark, like him. But they were not Ashanti. He suspected that they both were Ewe, which made him wary. But they were not like any Ewe he knew. They were like the dogs of his village, slithering around, tails between their legs, looking at the ground. Not really men at all.

How long, he thought, before he would become like them. But then the answer sprang to him: never. But his heart was heavy. He now wished that he had had the strength to die in the belly of the vessel. Because he was smart enough to realize that such as these two beaten men was what he would be expected to become here as well.

If needed, he would pretend to be what they wanted. But he would learn. He would learn where he was so that he could figure out how not to be here anymore.

* * * *

"Your name is Hubbard. On the plantation, you will simply be called Hubbard. Away from the plantation, you will be called Hubbard Semple, so that all know who you belong to."

I belong to no one but myself, Kweku declared inside. But to the overseer, he simply said, "Yas, Mas."

He had been in the field for two changes of the moon ere he had been called before the overseer. He had learned to cut the cane for the sugar, and he had been good at it. He was smart enough to know that he needed to be good at whatever he was told to do. And he was quick with the language, too. By the time the overseer summoned him, he was able to understand what having a new name meant—and he had quickly learned the phrase , "Yas, Mas."

He wasn't going to learn the phrase, "Yas, Missus," for a while—but not all that long, actually.

He didn't really see the plantation's master, Nathan Semple, again before he left Barbados. Semple spent a good amount of his time in Bridgetown, where Kweku's vessel had docked. But Semple's wife, Louise, didn't like the dirty bustle of Bridgetown.

She did, however, enjoy coming out to the verge of the trees bordering the cane fields, along with a chair carried by one of the house darkies. She brought her needlework with her and sat and watched the slaves, mostly men stripped to their waists and in leggings that barely covered their pelvises and thighs, work the cane.

"Starting today you will only work the fields from sunup to sundown," the overseer told Kweku when he'd been given his new name.

"Yas, Mas," Kweku—rather, Hubbard—said, his face pointed at the floor, his body held in a submissive position.

"And after you have supped, you will spend the nights in the huts I tell you to go to. And you will help increase the family of slaves on the plantation. Do you understand?"

"Yes, Mas."

Hubbard was determined to be good at what he was told to do. And he was very good with his work at night in the huts. He was so good that descriptions of his prowess and equipment reached the plantation house and the ears of Louise Semple.

One night Hubbard heard the quiet knock on the door of the hut he had been sent to that night. He had finished with his plowing and so could rise quickly and go to the door. Louise Semple was standing there in a night dress and holding a candle that was wavering in her hand.

"There is need of you in the big house," was all she said.

It was all she needed to say. Hubbard had seen her eyeing him, and he knew that both Massa Semple and the overseer had gone to Bridgetown for several nights. That was the first—but not the last—time that Hubbard was to use the phrase "Yas, Missus."

Hubbard might bow and scrape to the master and the overseer, but he could see immediately that he need not do so for the missus. He let her know he would fuck her, but he insisted that she bathe her body of the stink of all that she covered herself with by day before he would give her the cock. And in the giving of the cock he made very sure that she understood that this was being done for his pleasure.

Neither the overseer nor Nathan Semple were really sure that anything was happening If they had been, Hubbard would have been flayed and hung. Both he and Louise were too clever for that. Louise wasn't quite as clever as Hubbard, though— certainly not in the long run. In the short run she was much too happy that Nathan spent so much time in Bridgetown. She also spent entirely too much time on the lawn of the plantation near the cane fields. And her maids twittered behind their fingers at how often she bathed.

But Nathan couldn't be sure that anything at all was wrong—at least not then. There was that nagging feeling, however. Louise had become entirely too pleasant and no longer was anxious for the cock as she had previously been when he'd been away for an extended time. So, he went into Bridgetown and bought four strapping male slaves from an incoming vessel stopping in Barbados en route to Massachusetts, the slaver *Thomas*, captained by its owner, Thornton Cole, and struck up a deal quite favorable with Cole for a trade for four of the youngest and fittest slaves from Semple Hill.

Cole couldn't believe his good fortune. He was trading four recently transported slaves who might not even survive the night and were straight out of Africa for four healthy field hands.

He was even more delighted when the four slaves were brought to him from Semple Hill. One, in particular, because Thornton Cole had very special pleasures, was a wonder to see that put Cole immediately into arousal. When he asked, the Semple Hill overseer, who was more observant than his master was, was happy to identify the slave as Hubbard Semple—and to be well rid of him.

It was a slow progression up the East Coast of the American continent for the *Thomas*, but Hubbard was well away en route to a new life before Louise determined that she was pregnant and was faced with the dangerous chore of doing something about it—knowing full well who the father was.

* * * *

It didn't take Hubbard long to figure out what Thornton Cole was interested in during the voyage of the *Thomas* up the American coast. He was prepared to do what needed to be done to survive, but he'd also do what he could to bend the inevitable to his advantage. Hubbard was a smart young man. Okyere had been quite correct in the assessment that he needed to get rid of him back in the Ashanti Kingdom.

Barely two days out of Bridgetown, the slaver, Cole, showed that he was much more progressive than most of those transporting slaves from Africa to the New World. He didn't keep his merchandise cooped up in the dark hold of the ship—at least not all of the time. He had them brought up in small groups during the day and permitted them to stand, albeit still in chains, on the open deck and take in the clean, sea air. Those permitted to do this were fed while they were topside.

Hubbard had already seen the interested look in Thornton Cole's eyes on the dock back in Bridgetown. But now he gained more evidence of the man's interest. Nearly every time a group was brought up from the hold, Hubbard was among them, being given far more access to the unusual privilege than any of the other slaves. And while Hubbard stood there, filling his lungs as full as he could with fresh air—naked as all of the slaves were, except for their chains—he could see out of his peripheral vision that Cole was watching him. If he turned his face toward Cole, he would be rewarded with a friendly smile.

The clincher came in the late afternoon of the fourth day, as the *Thomas* hugged the coast and sailed north by northeast.

Hubbard was brought up to the deck with a group of others. However, he was separated from them. The others, along with most of the crew on deck were moved toward the bow. Hubbard was separated from the two men he'd been manacled to with leg irons and chains and was chained to an iron ring next to the window of a cabin at the bow. He was at the side railing, barely within sight of anyone else in the crew or the group of slaves brought up with him.

He enjoyed the solitude and was feeling the closest sense of freedom he had in over a year.

But while he was filling his lungs with sea air, as he always did when given the chance, and watching the American coast slide by in the distance, he heard the noise. He knew instantly what the noise was. He was a smart young man. And he'd been making that noise regularly himself in recent months.

He instinctively turned and looked through the window into the cabin beyond, as he obviously was meant to do.

There were several comely young men in the crew. Hubbard hadn't shown much interest in them, but a good part of him figuring out what made Thornton Cole tick was in watching Cole watch these young men.

The young man that Cole had naked and bent over his captain's chair in the cabin was one of the "prettier" young men of the crew, one who it didn't take much for Hubbard to figure out was providing sport to many of the men in the crew. Hubbard had already decided that this was probably exactly why the young man was part of the crew—for the sport the others needed as they plied the Atlantic and Caribbean with their endless stream of slaves.

Cole too was naked, and although he was fucking the ass of the young sailor hard from behind, he was standing somewhat away from him in all parts not buried in the young man. He was flexing his muscles, showing off his physique, which Hubbard thought was a fine physique, for a man. It was rather obvious,

Hubbard being a smart young man himself, that Cole was actually posing and even putting himself in the best light. And he was posing for the window Hubbard was looking through. He was posing for Hubbard, sending a message.

Hubbard got the message. He knew that Cole, as not only the ship's captain, but also its owner, and most likely the man who would hold sway over Hubbard's life even when they got to the auction block wherever they were going, was all-important to his own survival.

Therefore, he wasn't surprised that when the ship arrived off a port Cole happily told him was named Beaufort and was a short sloop sail from a newly building town named Savannah on a river of the same name, to find that most of the crew were getting into the ship's sloop.

Cole was pleased to tell Hubbard, who had been brought up from the hold, dowsed with water several times, and brought to Cole in his quarters, that he had given much of the crew a two-day furlough for a visit to this new town called Savannah. More than half of the slaves in the hold also were sent off with his men—for the slave markets of the south. But Hubbard wasn't among those sent away.

A short crew remained on the ship, and would come if Cole summoned them, but other than that he and Hubbard would be quite alone in Cole's cabin.

"How does that set with you?" Cole asked.

"Yes, Mas," Hubbard answered.

Cole took that as a hopeful sign. He was nearly salivating at the sight of the dark brown giant standing before him, legs proudly spread wide, low-hanging manhood and balls looking just as proud, naked, but for the wrist irons connected with a chain. He was wearing leg irons too, but there were no chains down there.

"Did you see me through the window the other evening?"

"Yas, Mas."

"Do you understand what I was doing?"

"Yas, Mas."

45

"I could find a hammock for you in the forecastle. You would not need to go back to the hold. Do you understand that? I can do that if you please me. Do you want to please me?"

"Yas, Mas." Hubbard could actually understand Cole quite well, and he also had a larger vocabulary in English than he had exhibited. But he wanted to keep it simple. There were not many choices here. He still could possibly obtain a better choice than Cole had in mind. He would have to play this carefully.

Cole came around his desk and approached the magnificent African. He circled Hubbard, poking and prodding and gliding his hands here and there. Thus far it was no more than any slaver had done on several occasions, starting at the river in Ashanti. Hubbard understood what would please Cole, though, and he thought whatever thoughts he had to think to make his member start to harden.

Cole gave a little pleased gasp, as Hubbard began to have some success with that.

The slaver's hands were trembling as they glided over Hubbard's muscles now, and he went down on his knees almost as if they'd given way. Hubbard grunted as he felt the wet mouth open up over the bulb of his cock. He stood there, for several minutes, lost in whatever thoughts were needed to give Cole the response he wanted.

Hubbard was guided over to the desk and shown that he was to bend over it on his belly and spread his legs. He grunted again, now genuinely in an arousal of his own, as Cole's tongue and lips moved between his butt cheeks and began giving his opening wet attention.

The African giant waited until Cole had risen, stripped, and was approaching his quarry's back with a hand holding his dick steady. And then, lightning swift, Hubbard rose, turned, and twisted Cole around and down on *his* belly on the desk top.

Cole would have cried out—if he could. But Hubbard had the chain running from one wrist to the other around Cole's neck, and although he wasn't choking the slaver hard, he was applying enough pressure to cause Cole to care about nothing but the next breath—and trying with his own frantic hands to pull the chain away from his throat.

46

He would have screamed if he could when Hubbard's cock began to invade his channel, but once it was past the sphincter and well lodged and Cole had time to adjust to the length and girth of it, Hubbard slowly pulled the chain away and Cole's gurgling noises turned to little yips of ecstasy.

Cole, who never before had been the one taken, was now completely taken. He had had no idea that his arousal and satisfaction was greater with another man's cock inside him than it had been with him doing the fucking. And this slave, this Hubbard Semple, had a magnificent black cock that sent Cole into waves and waves of satisfaction. Thornton Cole had moved into a whole new world of desire fulfilled.

That night Hubbard did not sleep either in the hold with the other slaves or in a hammock in the forecastle. He didn't sleep much at all. He spent the night in Cole's bed in the captain's cabin, giving Cole what he now realized he wanted more than anything else in sex and what would help Hubbard survive.

By the time they reached the coast of the Massachusetts Bay Colony, Hubbard was a fixture in Thornton Cole's cabin. He was out of his chains, washed regularly, and dressed as well as any of the crew whenever there was a reason for him to be dressed at all—which Cole did what he could to keep at a minimum.

He had also successfully signaled to Cole that he also needed to wash more regularly to realize the most satisfying servicing from Hubbard.

Standing off of the harbor at Shernhaven and waiting for the sloops to arrive to take Cole's precious human cargo to the wharf and the slave market, Cole stood beside Hubbard at the rails and worked with him to identify and name the steadily moving improvements being made to the town.

"That's a lighthouse up there—or will be when it's finished—on the Lower Head spit," Cole said. "And opposite to that on that bluff over there, the Upper Head, is my house. Not the one right on the bluff, but the next one down toward the town. And look how much has been built in the town since last time I was in port. Edwin Geer has been busy. I hope that he has been as diligent with adding to our tavern at the corner of Hobart and Cole. Yes, I own a tavern—along with Edwin Geer—on a street with my name on it. Geer has a street named for his family too—on the other side of the common. See where that is? See the shipyard in the shadow of Upper Head? Look to the right of that. To where you can see tree tops. That's the common. Aiken Shern wants that named for him. But we shall see about that."

While Cole was rambling on, the crew was in the hold trying to make the surviving slaves as presentable as possible for market. Already buyers were gathering on the wharf. Cole wanted to dispose of his goods as quickly as possible. He was lucky. Only five of them had died on the sail up from Barbados.

Hubbard was thinking lickety-split while Cole was talking even though he was trying to pay attention to and follow what Cole was explaining. If there was any hope of escape when they got to the town, what was pouring out of Cole's mouth was useful information.

The African feared what would happen. Who would buy him; what would be expected of him.

He needn't have worried, though. Thornton Cole had no intention of selling his big African stud. He didn't even have him landed on the wharf where buyers could see him. Two crew members took him—once more in chains, but dressed, to the south of the Lower Head spit, where Cole had horses sent to bring them around the Lower Head Road to Hobart Street and then to the corner of Cole and Hobart.

Hubbard saw that the biggest building in evidence on the street was the place Cole had told him about, the tavern Coles and Geer owned together, the tavern named the Landho, having inherited it from three generations of ancestors. The Landho had always been much more than a tavern.

Here, Hubbard was chained to a bed by an ankle and kept there for two months, earning Cole the money he had planned to get out of such a fine specimen of a slave.

Eventually, Hubbard became a fixture at the bar in the tavern. He was chained to the rail on the service side of the bar to act as a bartender and as a visual threat to troublemakers whenever he wasn't unchained and led upstairs with a customer—where he was chained again.

By night, he lived in the loft of the carriage house of the Cole home on the Upper Head bluff. He never entered the Cole house, where Thornton Cole's wife held sway, with her four children, three boys and a girl. But when Thornton Cole ordered a fancy mattress brought down from Boston, it was destined to go in the loft above the carriage house, not in the main house.

Thornton Cole spent few nights in his own house during the periods when he wasn't at sea building his slave trade business.

Cole didn't come back from one of these voyages; neither did his ship, the *Thomas*.

After a few months, Mrs. Cole, who didn't believe in slavery and who sold her husband's other two slaver ships, let Hubbard go free. She also freed the female kitchen slave Thornton had brought into the house. Hubbard continued to work in the tavern, another business Mrs. Cole divested herself of by selling it to Edwin Geer. Mrs. Cole didn't believe in what she knew was going on there either.

Hubbard and the kitchen maid produced six children before Edwin Geer caught Hubbard Semple trying to produce a child on his wife too.

Then Edwin Geer shot Hubbard Semple dead. That didn't make a ripple of concern in the town of Shernhaven, and Judge Aiken Shern dismissed all charges against Geer.

Hubbard Semple had been a popular figure in the town. Truth be known, Geer was the laughing stock of the town's men because his young wife was cuckolding him with far more than Semple and the townsmen liked to live vicariously in Semple's sexual exploits. But he was, after all, little more than a savage slave, and Edwin Geer was from a founding family, a family that had built the town almost with its own hands—although perhaps more with the Shern- and Cole-family brains.

There was some talk of burying Hubbard Semple in the corner of the commons, but by that time there was already a movement under foot to remove all of the graves there and rename the commons Shern Park.

Chapter Three: 1815

He felt the weight of his body pulling on his wrists where they were chained to the wall in the dungeon of the ritter's castle. His cheek rested against the clammy stone wall of the chamber. Still, though, the sweat was dripping down his brow and into his eyes. There was nothing he could do about that now.

Von Rostock had left him, saying he'd be back after refreshing himself.

If he stretched out his legs and perched on the balls of his feet, he could just manage to touch the cold, stone floor. He could only do this for a few moments, but it was great relief to his wrists when he did. And he could pull a bit away from the wall. The rough surface of the wall chafed him in his most tender spot when he wasn't pulled away from the surface.

It embarrassed him, but he couldn't help it. The ritter had laughed. Despite what the knight, the liege of Rostock, Mecklenburg, was doing to him, Peer was hard. No, he had to be honest, it was because of what the ritter was doing to him. His body had betrayed him. The harder the ritter punished his body, the deeper he moaned and the harder his cock became—robbing him of any attempt he could make to pretend that he didn't find the knight's attentions sexually arousing.

That was the mortification. Peer had enjoyed it. Even now, he was begging in his mind for Von Rostock to come back and resume the attentions.

In his wildest dreams a year earlier, Peer Fischer would not have guessed he would be in this dungeon—or even in this city. He had been a simple fisherman—in a long line of them, as his surname implied—in the seaside village of Ribnitz-Damgarten at the mouth of the Recknitz River, in Mecklenburg. Mecklenburg was one of the German duchies—on the north coast of Germany, separated from Denmark by the body of water known as the Mechlenburger Burcht, that made up the newly formed German Confederation. It was one of the weakest members of the confederation because it had been wracked by strife and inner conflict following the invasion and occupation by the French a decade earlier in the War of the Fourth Coalition.

Ribnitz-Damgarten was under the sway of the Hanseatic city of Rostock, but it was located almost equidistant between Rostock and another Hanseatic city, Stralsund. And beyond Rostock was the independent imperial city of Lubeck.

All of this existed as the source of intrigue and complex political maneuvering, exacerbated by a cruel and ruthless ruler in Rostock, the Ritter Horst von Rostock, who had not outgrown the pleasure of engaging in the war with Napoleon's armies and, indeed, existed to prepare for fighting and to fight. He also famously liked his sport—sport of the most exotic kinds.

Where this involved Peer Fischer was that, despite working in a vital occupation as a fisherman and living an isolated life in a small fishing village, he also had come of age to serve in the ritter's armed forces. All men of a certain age were expected to serve, and, as liege of all people in the Rostock district of the Duchy of Mecklenburg, Ritter Horst von Rostock would have his due—in whatever respect he demanded it.

Peer had led a quiet life in Ribnitz-Damgarten, but not necessarily a happy one. He did love the fishing, but at the end of each evening he had to return to his home, where he lived with his parents and their parents as well in a cottage not large enough for them. Work was, as a matter of fact, heavenly in the few months before he was forcibly enlisted in the ritter's army.

Peer's father was a cruel man. He beat his wife and he beat his children, and, if the village had allowed it, he would have beaten his parents as well. When he was fishing with Peer, Peer felt the lash on his back almost continuously. The lashing didn't cut too deeply—Peer's father wasn't about to disable his primary worker—but they were ever there. Peer came to expect them, almost, perversely, to seek them out to make him feel alive. Embarrassingly, as he came into his manhood, he found that the lashings also were arousing to him and could have been seen on the responses by his body if he had not concealed them.

He didn't really understand the connection between the slight pain and pleasure until Peer had reached conscription age and his father had decided not to go to sea anymore and to let Peer and his two younger brothers take over the fishing boat and the responsibility for the family's livelihood.

The two brothers of Peer were hardly old enough to go to sea when the ritter's guard had come through the town and conscripted the demanded number of recruits, a tally that included Peer. The loss of Peer's work at this time was devastating to the family's prosperity, but the family would just have to survive somehow without him.

Peer never did take to the soldiering, but, as he had worked his body well as a fisherman and was fair of countenance, if not overly tall, and with a ready, shy smile, he had caught the ritter's attention in the ranks, and soon found himself on the ritter's own personal guard force. The life in this force was not too demanding—and, in fact, the guard members had to devise extra sports to keep themselves in fighting fettle.

One of the ritter's favorite sports was wrestling. And because of his other pleasures, the sport took on elements not normally encountered in wrestling.

The ritter, himself, was a champion wrestler—at least the members of the guard made him so. In a match, the wrestlers would wrestle to exhaustion or until one could claim victory over the other by not only subjugating his spirit but by subjugating his body as well.

The wrestlers enjoyed their sport in the nude, and the mark of a victor was one who could encase his cock in the channel of the other and climax before the other could break the controlling hold.

The ritter loved to win, and, of course, his guard made sure that he did. But he also wanted at least the appearance of winning by right, so any wrestler who went up against him was either seasoned in the sport—or not seasoned at all and still a virgin to all things connected with the sport. This also was a pleasure the ritter enjoyed taking.

When Peer joined the guard, he most certainly wasn't seasoned in the sport. And as much as the demands of fishing that had been laid upon him were, he was a virgin to all facets of the sexual, other than the unusual arousal he got from mild applications of the lash.

He lasted ten minutes with the ritter on the wrestling mat, with the rest of the well-picked guardsmen gathered around and cheering the sport on. Peer had the strength, but he didn't have the technique and he didn't have the holds. He had also been advised that he did not want to win a wrestling match with the ritter, who had no sense of humor whatsoever. Still, the pain of the initial entry up his channel of the ritter's victory sword as Peer lay on his belly with his arms pinned behind his back and his legs entwined by those of the ritter prompted him to writhe and struggle, which the ritter enjoyed as he gained increased depth. Then with Peer moaning and groaning and, eventually, subsiding into grunts and sighs and the involuntary movement of his hips to aid in the plumbing of the depths, the ritter's victory was complete. Satisfied and satiated, the ritter rose from the matting, patted Peer on the bare buttocks, and pronounced that he was well pleased with the initiation.

After that Peer was paired twice with a man nearer his age and size, Klaus Reuter, who had been a jeweler's assistant before being conscripted. Klaus won both times—and took his victory both times. By now Peer was so resigned to it—and even catching on to the act enough—that the two frequently found themselves fucking in dark corners when they were able to manage it and even without the sham of sport.

As Peer became more acclimated to being in the Ritter's guard, he also became bolder and more curious about the life in the castle. One afternoon his curiosity got the best of him. He was roaming down a corridor in the upper basement of the castle when he came upon a chamber where vast amounts of amber were set out on a wooden table, presumably for inventory.

Peer knew what amber was. The area of Rostock he came from was famous for mining it, but mere peasants, of course, weren't permitted to have it. Any found went straight into the treasuries of the Ritter of Rostock and the Duke of Mecklenburg. But here, before him, lay several fortunes worth of it.

He didn't actually move into the chamber and touch any of it, but he certainly had been thinking of doing so. So, when a couple of other members of the guard accosted him, he looked as guilty as any thief.

The humorless ritter was not amused—at first. He roared at Peer when the young man was brought before him, and, in his anger, he commanded that the Fischer be stripped and bent over a barrel with strong men on each side holding his arms out while the ritter gave him a lashing on his back.

Not far into the punishment, however, the ritter stopped and now laughed—because he saw that his lashings were causing Peer's cock to harden and the young man to pant in an arousing mood well beyond pain.

This intrigued and aroused the ritter as well. So, that was how Peer Fischer came to be hung from chains by his wrists high on the wall of the castle dungeon and to have Ritter Horst von Rostock, also aroused now, standing behind him, working his own cock with one hand and flogging Peer with measured strokes with a whip held in the other hand.

After raising a bit of blood on Peer's back, the ritter came in close, licked the wounds and, reaching through Peer's spread legs, began to milk Peer's cock. Peer moaned for him.

"You like that, *ja*?"

Peer didn't answer. He just whimpered and wriggled his buttocks as the ritter started playing at his hole with the butt end of his whip.

"*Ich sprach. Es ist gut, ja*? Tell me. You like that, *ja*?"

"*Ja*," Peer answered with a low sigh. He couldn't fool the ritter; the ritter could feel in his grasp of Peer's hard cock that this aroused him. In fact, to Peer's surprise and embarrassment, he realized that he was aroused more by being bound to the wall than with the light flogging he had received. He'd had hints of this when the ritter and Klaus pinned him on the wrestling mat before taking him, but he hadn't fully understood what was arousing him at the time.

"Then *vielleicht*—perhaps—you like this even more. *Ja*?"

"*Ach, mein Got. Ach, Ja. Ja, ja, ja.*" Peer cried out his painful pleasure as the ritter lifted the young man's hips, set the tip of his cock between Peer's buttocks cheeks, thrust . . . and kept on thrusting, up, up, up inside him. Opening, stretching, punishing, getting into a rhythm that made Peer cry out at each deep thrust and moan at each contraction, then thrusting his buttocks back, begging for the next thrust.

The ritter laughed when Peer ejaculated against the stone wall. And after he was finished, he slapped Peer on the buttocks and said he was off to watch a wrestling match with the guards and would be back to punish Peer again in the way that he seemed to be taking so much pleasure from.

The ritter gone to his other sport for the day, Peer hung his head and tried to regularize his breath, mortified that he was enjoying this.

He stiffened at the feel of a hand on his back and the coolness of a wet rag on his welts. He turned his head.

"Klaus."

"Shhh, *Nicht*. Don't. Don't speak. They are all at the wrestling match, and I must be gone back to them before they realize I have left. I will free you. But then you will have to be a fugitive. You will have to escape beyond the reach of the ritter. He will be furious."

Peer said no more. He let Klaus release him and then he stumbled to a sitting position on the ground and rubbed his wrists and worked out the stretched muscles in his shoulders and arms. When he looked up, Klaus was gone.

He stole out of the castle then, but in looking for clothes to put on his back and boots for his feet, he once again stumbled upon the forbidden chamber with the mounds of amber in it.

There are more fortunes here than the ritter needs, Peer thought. And he owes me for the sport.

When Peer left the castle walls, it was with a heavy sack of amber on his back.

He headed for Lubeck, the nearest jurisdiction not controlled by the ritter and a place where he could find a vessel sailing to someplace where he could change the amber into gold.

There was no way for him to do it in Germany. Buyers could only deal with the ritter or the duke.

A cheap Lubeck inn on the evening before Peer was to leave on a vessel bound for England, as a crew member, was where Klaus found him.

"How did you find me?"

"Where else would you go?" Klaus said. "And the ritter and his guard will think on that too as soon as he realizes some of his amber is gone. You took that too, *nicht wahr*—not true?"

"*Ja*. But why are you here."

"To go with you, if I can. I did not get to the wrestling before I realized that the ritter would know who freed you. So, we are both hunted men."

"We will do our own hunting together then," Peer said, with a smile.

* * * *

Half way across the Atlantic to the young United States, a country fresh from having repelled the English a second time, Peer and Klaus enjoyed a comfortable cabin thanks to Klaus's talent in changing amber into gold in the jewelry markets of London. In this cabin, Peer learned that he enjoyed sex the most with his hands bound over his head to the brass slats in the headboard and his lover working diligently between his spread thighs.

"What can we do in the New World?" Klaus had asked when they were deciding what to invest their new fortune in.

"Well they do eat fish, I would guess," Peer answered. "And there are women there, so there will always be the need for baubles. I will satisfy one with the boat we buy and you can satisfy the other with a shop we buy."

"But where will be go? I hear about places like Boston and New York."

"Too large for a proper fishing village," Peer said. "We are Deutscher—Germans. I have asked where the Germans are going. Many are going to a place called Broad Bay, north of that big city named Boston. We keep with the Deutschers. We go to Broad Bay too."

So, that's where they headed when their ship landed in New York City.

And it was here that Peer Fischer bought his first fishing boat and Klaus Reuter opened his small jewelry shop.

One of Klaus's first customers was a woman named Mary Geer, visiting friends from a small coastal harbor town south of Boston. Mary liked the jewelry Klaus had in his store. She liked even more the friend of Klaus, that handsome fisherman, Peer Fischer, and she timed her visits to the shop that Klaus and Peer lived above to the times she saw that Peer's fishing boat was in the Broad Bay harbor.

Mary was a compassionate, steady, and resourceful woman. When Klaus took sick, rather than go back to her hometown of Shernhaven at the end of the summer, she stayed around to help out with Klaus's shop. She was happy to do so. But it needed close attendance. Klaus was so ill that Peer could not bed with him when he came back from his fishing trips. But Peer was a lustful person now and he had his needs. Mary had her desires, and she was an open minded, resourceful woman.

When Klaus became extremely ill and bedridden, Mary, who was attentive to Klaus's personal needs and to his shop, managed to have time left over to attend to Peer's basic needs too.

Peer moved into Mary's bed. And when Klaus died, Mary Geer and Peer were wed, the jewelry shop was sold—for a nice profit—and the wedded pair sailed south from Broad Bay to Mary's town of Shernhaven, where Mary Fischer assured Peer there was room for another fishing company and where she had an old family home high on a bluff overlooking the town. She had it all to herself most of the time now, as her brother had moved the headquarters of the family construction business up to Boston. Here Mary opened a jewelry shop of her own.

* * * *

Peer delighted as he approached the mouth of Shernhaven harbor. It had all he could ask for. The newly completed Lower

Head lighthouse on the cliff at the end of the spit nearly encircling the harbor was the best along the coast as of date and would be one that he could keep in view for most of the fishing he would do. The harbor itself was perfectly formed, with docks and a wharf to the south—with, it appeared, plenty of available slip space. He already was planning for more boats, and there was a shipyard right there, below his house, that could make whatever fishing boat he wanted. Klaus hadn't had any heirs that Peer knew about and, anyway, the jewelry store had been purchased out of what Peer himself had stolen—ahem, taken as his due—from the castle of Ritter Horst van Rostock. So, Peer set out to double and then triple the size of his fishing venture almost as soon as he and his wife landed in Shernhaven.

Peer Fischer had worried about getting established and obtaining slip space and setting up a market for his fish. It had not been all that easy to do in Broad Bay. Shernhaven was an established town, settled by the English. And he was a foreigner. Surely the fishing industry here would be protective of those already here. But his wife, Mary, had told him not to worry about that. And from the moment she pointed for him to look where their house was, on the heights of the Upper Head, his worry began to dissipate.

Within days, he found confirmation that the Geer name—even when wedded to another—opened doors in Shernhaven. And within weeks he discovered that in the ocean beyond the mouth of the Shernhaven harbor, but within sight of the Lower Head lighthouse, all of the cod, haddock, pollack, tuna, and sea bass he could ever want nearly jumped into his boat. Within months he launched his second boat, built in the convenient and bustling shipyard inside the harbor and at the base of the Upper Head heights. He had been treated quite deferentially by old Alden Shern, the patriarch of the Shern Shipyard, which was quite heartening considering that Judge Shern was the town's leading figure, and also quite attentively by the judge's achingly handsome and dark and mysterious son, Adney. From everything that was going his way, Peer was in seventh heaven and on his way.

Peer wasn't in ninth heaven yet, but he was so grateful for the blessing that had come into his life that he could be patient—and could be forgiving if life never fully gave him what he needed.

Mary was a dutiful and devoted wife, and a perfect and fecund mother. But Peer had been to the limits of certain sexual tastes. If he never had tasted them, he probably could have been fully content with Mary and his new life in Shernhaven. But he *had* tasted them.

He almost had subsided into "oh well" complacency when he overheard mention of the Landho tavern at the intersection of Hobart and Cole Streets—and suggestions of what might be obtained there.

He already had seen—and been fascinated by—the three strapping Semple sons who had arrested his attention when strolling through the newly named and landscaped Shern Park in the center of the town. They were so exotic and large and well-formed that he couldn't avoid taking a second look at them and speculating on what could be. That they were as black as black could be only intrigued him more. He hadn't seen anything like that back in Germany, and although he's seen a few black slaves in Broad Bay, the Semple men didn't act like slaves. They stood tall and proud and walked like they had superior manhood between their legs—which made Peer speculate that perhaps they did.

He sensed that Solomon Cole, who owned the banking institution recently opened in a building facing Shern Park, was one with him—secretly interested in more than a woman's skirt. Cole had signaled as much to him a few times until it became obvious to him that both he and Peer were interested in the same sort of man. They lost direct sexual interest in each other then, but upon identifying a kindred spirit, Cole became a rich source of information, albeit obliquely provided, on the aspects of Shernhaven that few talked about.

Peer knew of no one else he could confide in even in indirect terms with less risk than Solomon Cole. He figured that he could innocently mention the Landho tavern and easily withdraw in feigned surprise if Cole told him bluntly that the upper rooms of the Landho provided exactly what Peer—

nervously and with a great deal of guilt and embarrassment but also much pent up frustration—was looking for.

When Peer mentioned it while in the bank arranging transfer of the money for the boat near completion at the Shern Shipyard, Solomon Cole laughed and leaned across the desk at him, with perhaps a little leer in his eye, and whispered, "I would be pleased to take you there to see what it is for yourself. But I would think you would have no need for that."

"No need?"

"No. You own it, you know."

"Own it? Own what?"

"The Landho. Your wife, Mary, hasn't told you? It's just one of many Geer family holdings in the town. I assumed you knew—That Mary kept it for you because . . . it would pleasure you."

After that he never looked at Mary the same way again. What did she know about the nature of the Landho tavern, he wondered? In fact, what had she known about him and Klaus when she had moved into the upper rooms of the jewelry store in Broad Bay? It was all too much for Peer to fathom—and there, of course, was no proper way for him to ask Mary. There were some things even a husband and wife—especially a husband and wife—didn't discuss at the opening of the nineteenth century.

But after a year of Mary and just Mary and when she had birthed their first child, a son, and was so taken with motherhood that Peer could have told her that he was sailing to the moon and would be gone three weeks, she just would have smiled and wished him a safe journey, Peer built up the courage to enter the Landho tavern.

By then everyone in town knew who Peer Fischer was—and all of them had probably known that the Geers, the family he'd married into, owned the place when he hadn't known it for so long.

So, there was not so much as a twitter when he went in. The bar room was crowded; the atmosphere was not just boisterous, it was downright bawdy; and those pushing the drinks and pulling men up the stairs by their hands were both female and male—and dressed skimpily and suggestively.

One of the Semple boys was tending bar, and Peer almost turned and walked back outside.

But he'd entered and everyone had seen him, so leaving at this point would only be both unsatisfying and a bit too late for him to pretend innocence to what went on between these walls.

After a few drinks, during which the Semple boy obviously wanted Peer to let him know exactly what his pleasure was, Peer nodded his head toward a big bruiser who was trying to convince a man to go upstairs with him. He looked like particularly rough trade and he was cradling a hand whip, which was just about all the statement of his wares that anyone would need.

Before he could do more than gesture, though, Peer felt a nudge at his elbow and he turned to see, in shock, that the younger Shern he had been dealing with at the shipyard, Adney, was now sitting beside him and looking very interested. He had leather wrists bands, tight-fitting shirt and trousers, and a thick chain around his neck.

"If that's what you want, I can help you with that," the young Shern whispered to Peer. "The walls here are rather thin, and that isn't the best pleasure for here. I have someplace we could be more private."

The "someplace" proved to be the loft of a livery stable, across from Solomon Cole's bank. The stable was closed because the Geers had built a larger, much-better-outfitted stable next door to put the independent owner of this business out of business. The younger Shern had bought the building for a song.

His special den was in the loft area, with old hay bales cushioning the sound on the front and two side walls and heavy iron rings set at intervals along the back walls at different heights. Peer wasn't tall, but there was a set positioned just within his grasp. The outfitting of Adney's lofty retreat immediately reminded Peer of the ritter's dungeon and caused him to respond in a way that made young Adney Shern laugh and run the strands of his horse whip lovingly through his hands. Peer already was naked and his interest in what Adney had in mind already was obvious to both of them.

Peer had never seen a small rubber ball on strappings such as Adney produced as he prodded Peer toward the back wall. But he soon learned what that was for.

Adney had Peer strung up in no time and did lip and tongue play between his buttocks cheeks that Peer had never experienced before and that was driving him crazy—until he learned that the rubber ball in his mouth was for biting hard on as, though memories of the ritter and his dungeon came back to Peer, these memories made the ritter out to be a midget in contrast to Adney in the staff that was being shoved up inside him after he'd been flogged and almost exhausted from writhing.

Now he was in ninth heaven.

Chapter Four: 1849

John Dungan, the third son of Archibald, the Baron de Blaguere, of Ardkill, Londonderry, was a man of few words but of precipitous action. When the Irish potato famine started destroying the lives and working ability of the families producing the Irish whiskey at his family's distillery in Londonderry—and particularly in challenging his endurance at watching families that had worked for his for generations starve—John took action.

John started by pleading to his father, the baron, who was an admiral in Her Majesty's Royal Navy, and to his two older brothers, one just recently having arrived in India with the Queen's 70th Surrey Regiment and the other a Catholic prelate in Boston in England's former American colony of Massachusetts. All entreaties that John made to his family to bring help in to aid the starving employees and families that had made the family rich had produced little more than offers of prayer from Boston.

John was smart enough to know that, as religiously faithful as the people of Londonderry were, prayers from far-off Boston weren't going to save them if their own prayers didn't. You can't eat prayers, the practical side of him screamed out to him. You also can't eat money. John's family had plenty of it. But if he couldn't get it translated into something his workers could eat—and so widespread was the famine that all efforts he made in this direction were to no avail—then "wealth" was useless. It was useless to try to wrest it from the grip of his father and brothers anyway.

His father's response was that he was sure John had the intelligence and resourcefulness to work the problem out on his own. This was not exactly carte blanche from the head of the family, but who knew, John thought, where the edge of using his resourcefulness was.

When the situation with the potato blight seemed like it could not get any worse and be survived, John's intelligence and resourcefulness kicked in. He took action—on his own without further consultation with his father or brothers. His studied assessment was that you couldn't find a meal where no food was to be had at any price. He made an offer to any of the families of the distillery workers who would take him up on the venture. He would pay their passage to America upon two-week's notice if they were to agree to work with him for ten years beyond that in reestablishing the family liquor business in America.

Few were willing to leave Ireland, the hardships they had always known making them feel safer than the unknown, but enough did for John to believe he could start anew in Boston. And although he could suffer regret for those who didn't go, he would not suffer guilt, as he had given them a choice. He did not pull their jobs from underneath them; he left the Londonderry distillery in the hands of a capable and faithful master distiller who had, regretfully, said he was too old to go and that his wife was too sick to survive the voyage.

The ship, the *Washington,* sailed from Dublin to New York City in the fall of 1849, and by Christmas of that year, John Duggan had established his Irish whiskey distillery in Boston. It was a year of a great migration from Ireland to the United States, with more Irishmen going to Boston than anywhere else. And Irishmen were pleased to have access to the same Irish whiskey they enjoyed in Londonderry.

John Dungan's business thrived, and he soon was being invited within the hallowed circle of Boston society. That he could bring the liquor to events definitely worked in his favor.

Irish and construction went hand in glove in Boston, and it wasn't long before John met up with and began to socialize with the Geer family, which was prominent in the region's construction industry. Samuel Geer, the patriarch of that family, took a particular interest in the solidly built, sandy-haired young man who was so strikingly gifted with ruggedly handsome looks and so recently arrived from Londonderry, where Geer's sources had ferreted out the Dungan family's barony. No one in America, of course, had any idea that the third son of an Irish baron had little inherent worth—beyond his own intelligence and resourcefulness.

John only figured out Samuel's especial interest when Samuel's sister, a widow named Mary on indefinite visit to the core family in Boston, constantly showed up to the events he was invited to and usually was seated next to him.

Mary was a comely, plump woman, if a bit long in the tooth. And she was an engaging conversationalist. The only aspect to her that took John a bit aback, perhaps, was that she sometimes could be surprisingly earthy in a conversation. She also was a bit forward. But that part John didn't mind so much—especially when opportunities arose for the two to be quite alone and Mary became amorous. In the dark, Mary's treasures were no worse than any other lasses, and her long-in-the-tooth disadvantages quickly were turned into talented courtesan delights.

John might be a devout Catholic, but he wasn't married—and didn't intend to be anytime soon—and Mary was a willing widow. And he was not a eunuch.

He didn't even think of marriage—no matter how much Mary and her brother lauded the glories of it—until the day his brother, the prelate, the second son of the Baron de Blaguere, invited him to dinner.

John should have known something was wrong. The priest didn't often invite him to dinner—and certainly didn't entertain him as lavishly as he was doing on this evening. And the prelate most certainly didn't attend upon him as closely as he had done through the meal. Ever since John had arrived in Boston—and started attending the masses conducted by his brother in the huge cathedral he had at his command—his brother had required a new introduction nearly every time they came together and even then peered at John as if he just might be some distant relation from across the pond, but possibly not, as there were so many Dungans in Londonderry.

"I do be having a letter from Father," the priest delicately set forth over coffee and cigars.

"Ah, do ya now?" John responded, not yet on guard. "And what be he up to now, can ya say? Well, is he? Still on the sea?"

"The letter be for ya, John."

"Oh?"

And it was. The letter thanked John for his resourcefulness in moving the distillery to America and, he understood, already turning a good profit with it. There were only a few jabs about walking off with part of the family fortune without permission. But the bottom line was that the baron's first son was now leaving his army post in India and had a hankering for moving to the States rather than back to still-starving Ireland.

And he would be taking over the reins of the family distillery in Boston now.

John Dungan and Mary Geer Fischer were married in the Catholic cathedral in Boston in the fall of 1850. Mary had been visibly displeased at the requirement to become Catholic herself, a consideration that harkened her back to her English ancestors' public aversion to the Catholic Church. Charles I, who had given the land grants for her native town in Massachusetts, was educated as a Scottish Presbyterian and became a devout high Anglican. Those who had received his favor by way of land grants had fallen into step with him on that. The first permanent building erected in the land grant town the Geers had settled in had been an Anglican church. However, when John's brother pointed out that John could only marry a Catholic and that was that, Mary quickly came around. Mary had always been quite good at hiding her true feelings and activities if there was an advantage to it. And having been bedded already by the young, handsome, highly sensual, and virile John Dungan, the widow Mary definitely saw the advantages to the marriage. Mary and her brother had worked too hard for this prize to let it slither off of the hook.

John Dungan had no heart to stay in Boston where the company he had built with his own labor and sweat—but, unfortunately, with his father's money—had been snatched from his hands. And, mission accomplished, Mary was anxious to get home to her own town, Shernhaven, a harbor town fourteen miles to the south of Boston, and her brother, Silas, also mission accomplished, was equally anxious for her visit to come to a close.

Mary assured John that there would be plenty he could do in Shernhaven. He could even open a distillery if he wanted to. Although making whiskey had been his life, John no longer had an appetite for that business. The techniques and processes and formulas he knew all belonged to the house of Blaguere, and John knew that if he started another distillery, it only would be taken back by his father and older brother.

He initially was happy with Shernhaven. It was a delightful small town, with a perfect harbor and a thriving shipyard and fishing business at its foundation. The views from the Geer mansion, one of three on the heights of the Upper Head bluff overlooking the town and harbor, were delightful. John enjoyed no view better than one of business prosperity.

After a few months of being an instant member of a town founding family, however, John began to see a not-so-fine underbelly of the quaint, sparkling town. He couldn't really place his finger on it, but there was a tension here and hostile or knowing looks, and, when he paid attention, it seemed that everyone walking on the streets of town automatically was placing everyone he or she passed in the pecking order of things—and also assigning connections of seemly or unseemly habits. Perhaps it was just the small town atmosphere of it—a place where the same number of families had interacted since the time of inception. But, no, that didn't explain it either. He had come from just such a town—Londonderry—himself.

But, maybe, he thought, it was just that his own family had been so "above it" and isolated in Londonderry that it went on there too and he just hadn't caught onto it while he was there. It certainly wasn't like Boston, where virtually everyone was new—except for the Boston elite, which acted like it wasn't from Boston at all.

Then came the day, however, at a party at one of the other houses on the Upper Head, the Shern house, when John began to understand the nature of the underlying tension in the town—and started his journey of revulsion and rejection.

The party was a major campaign contributors sort of affair, where an election chest was being formed for the reelection of the area's delegate to the Massachusetts's assembly. This delegate was none other than Adney Shern, himself, the most prominent citizen of the town and the owner of the Shern Shipyard.

John had gone out on the terrace overlooking the town and was allowing himself to be mesmerized by the revolving light in the Lower Head lighthouse, when Adney Shern himself came out onto the terrace. They conversed for a short time before Shern, all self-assurance, began moving into a conversation that made John quite uncomfortable.

"Mary is a lucky woman, John," Adney said. "You are quite a handsome and alluring man. I'm sure, as the son of a baron and with your looks and build, you must have cut quite a swath in Ireland with . . ."

"I donna kin as that . . ." John stammered out, realizing that Adney had been nudging ever closer to him at the rail running at the edge of the cliff.

" . . . the lasses . . . and perhaps with the lads too. I can see how you might have had your pick."

Seeing that John was discomforted, Adney pulled back on the innuendo. But, being used to getting whatever he wanted, he returned to it after a brief discussion of town politics. When he asked John what his favorite sex toys were and if he was aroused by any particular discipline toys, John retreated as best he could into the house, where all of the other guests were gathered, some John now didn't doubt, knowing full well what had been offered out on the terrace. It was with great horror that it was beginning to dawn on him that there was much more burbling under the surface with the town leaders than his straightforward, simple assessments had discerned.

From this point forward, John couldn't think of Shernhaven without thinking of this underbelly that disgusted him.

And as well as being a straight-laced, devout man, John was also a man who wanted purpose and action in his life. There was only so much thrill a young man can get out of watching the town and harbor bustle from above in the day, following the rotation of the lighthouse at the end of the spit of the Lower Head in the twilight, and plowing your grasping old wife at night. John soon wanted to be productive once more—something that he doubted he'd ever be with Mary at her age—although she was to surprise him in ensuing years with popping out two sons of his own—or at least he hoped they were his own.

"What is it you want to do, John?" Mary asked when he brought the subject up one night. "We could use a distillery, but you've already said you can't do that. But the Geers have other businesses here. You could take over the management of any of those. The coach service to Boston and Braintree, for instance. Or our local branch of the construction trade. I wouldn't wish to give over my own dalliance with the jewelry store, of course. There's the fishing concern, but that was a favorite of my first husband's, and my sons with him would not be pleased to lose control over that—or to welcome in another opinion on how they should operate the business. And there's the Landho, of course."

"I dinna know, Mary. It must be something, ya know. What is this Landho ya talk of now?"

"Why, haven't I spoken of it before? It's the tavern down at the corner of Hobart and Coles. I don't have much to do with it other than receive an accounting of the revenues, which are considerable. I have the Semple family managing it—you know that family of freed slaves with the powerfully built and handsome young men who do much of the work around the town."

"A tavern, ya say? Where they do serve liquor?"

"Yes, yes, of course. And that's something you know well about, isn't it? Dealing with liquor. You wouldn't have to make it. You could reestablish your business interests by selling it."

"Who might I talk to about this tavern business now?"

"Well, there's Silas Cole at the Cole banking house on Shern Park. He handles the finances on all of the Geer businesses in town. I could write up a letter for him assigning all decisions on the tavern to you. And then at the tavern, it would probably be Henry Semple. I think he's the Semple brother who is managing that from day to day."

"Perhaps that would be a good start. Ya will write the letter?"

"Yes, yes, certainly. But first, I am in a mood. Perhaps we can go upstairs."

Mary was always in the mood. But sometimes in order to make sure John was in the mood, she made little hints like this that certain favors led to other favors. In this instance, the calendar indicated that this favor led to their first son.

* * * *

Silas Cole wasn't at the bank when John Dungan rode his horse down the Upper Head road to where it connected with Wharf Street and then turned right on Braintree to Shern Park. He was told that Cole was at the Landho tavern. This was fine with John. He could see Cole and the tavern's proprietor, Henry Semple, at the same time.

This is what he did—but not quite the way he'd imagined he'd be seeing them.

One of the first things he saw when he entered the tavern, which was surprising because there were so many such disturbing sights to look at that were a shock to him, was his stepson, Garen Fischer. Garen should have been out in one of his fishing boats— and perhaps he had been earlier in the day. But now he was in the tavern and sitting at the bar.

His head snapped around as if someone had said something to him when John appeared at the door. The first expression John saw on his stepson's face was one of fear and consternation, but then his eyes narrowed and he gave a little smile.

John saw that there was a big bruiser of a man sitting next to and quite close to Garen at the bar with a hand on Garen's shoulder. John didn't know what to make of that, but something down deep inside him was disturbed and was screaming at him that he didn't like what he saw. He didn't have long to look at Garen, though, who was of age and could be drinking in a bar if he wanted to be. There was so much else going on around the bar room to disturb John. Scantily clad women. Scantily clad men, for

70

that matter. Loose-morals-looking men and women. And a lot of glassy-eyed men, some of whom were sitting a lot closer to each other than John found comfortable. And some of them with hands not where John would think they belonged. Entirely too much electricity in the air for John.

He strode over to the bar and spoke in a demanding voice to the bar keep, a jet-black young man, who might be a Semple, but who looked to be too young to be the Semple John was looking for. "I be John Dungan, owner of the tavern. I come to talk to the manager, Henry Semple. Ya not be him, by any chance? And Silas Cole. I be told he be here as well."

"Upstairs; last door on the right," the young black man answered, looking at the glass he was polishing, not particularly impressed with John's declaration of authority.

"Which man?" John asked.

"Both," came back the answer.

John shot a look in Garen's direction but then looked away quickly. Garen was being embraced by the bigger man and his chin was being cupped in the man's hand and turned away from John.

I'll tend to that later, John thought, as he started up the stairs to the rooms above. But even then he didn't know in what way he would tend to that. It certainly wasn't something he felt he could mention to Mary. And the young man was her son, not his.

Garen turned his head, pulling out of the grasp of the other man, if only temporarily, and saw his stepfather climbing the stairs. He gave a little smile. He would have never known, he thought. Perhaps . . .

The door to the last room on the right down the hall on the second floor wasn't fully shut, so John didn't knock. Later he wished that he had done so.

He had found Silas Cole and Henry Semple. They were stretched out on a single bed in a room that was bare save for the bed, a straight chair, and a small bureau with a basin with pitcher and a small stack of towels on top of it. The single window looked out at the back of the building behind the tavern, toward Wharf Street. A dismal view of a fetid alley was all it provided. But, then,

71

John didn't suppose anyone came into this room for the view out of the window.

Both men were naked. Henry, a gigantic, heavily muscled black stud, was stretched behind Silas, cupping Silas's back into his stomach. He had an arm under Silas's belly, with a hand on Cole's hard cock, and he was lifting Silas's leg with his other hand.

Even from where John stood at the door, he could see that a good portion of an immense cock was inside Cole's ass—and both Cole's hips and Semple's pelvis were moving in a rhythm that John's appearance at the door didn't interrupt a stroke.

Cole's eyes were hooded in lust and satisfaction.

"I have Henry till four," he said. "Come back then, John, if you want a taste of what I'm enjoying."

Silas knew who John Dungan was. And he hadn't shown a bit of surprise or concern that John was there at the door. This perhaps shocked John the most at that point, a shock that surmounted what already had been a highly shocking ten minutes. He turned without a word and descended the stairs. He would take care of this later. There was a lot to take care of—later after he'd regained control of his composure.

His shock increased as he reached the bottom of the stairs. The room was still in a boisterous, lustful swirl, but John had no trouble picking his stepson out. Garen and the ominous man he was with—a rough boat builder John remembered seeing carrying heavy loads in the shipyard—had moved to a table near a corner. Garen was facing John, but he wasn't seeing him. His head was bent back to the face of the other man by the man's hand on Garen's throat. Garen was sitting on the man's lap, facing away from him. They were kissing. Garen was not wearing trousers now. His legs were bare. From the movement John could see of the two men's bodies, there was no doubt what was inside Garen's ass and what it was doing there.

Unable to speak, John turned and walked out of the tavern.

But John wasn't only a man of high morals; he also was a man of determination. Within three weeks, he was spending nearly his full time at the tavern, which already had been renamed Dungan's. The Semples had been dismissed, as had been all of the

72

loose-looking women and men he'd seen there on his first visit. While he was looking for trustful and competent barmen, he was tending the bar himself.

He actually was enjoying getting back in touch with the world of liquor and had already arranged a cut-rate price with his own family's distillery, which brought an Irish liquor to Shernhaven that the hedonist town he was slowly becoming fully aware of lapped up like milk. Business had slacked off by the redirection of it, but it was still good—all because of the popularity of the Blaguere brand of whiskey.

With Mary's permission, he engaged the local Geer construction company to completely redo the tavern, which was a hodge-podge of ancient, shoddy construction and haphazard add-ons. The main structure was two stories, but it had expanded to the side lot, where there were two other stories composed of a warren of small rooms, the function of which had been made shockingly and quickly apparent to John on his first visit to the tavern.

He had the side building torn down, and he sold the lot at a profit, which helped keep Mary quiet against the many private complaints she received about the changes at the tavern. Being the good businesswoman she was, she merely provided another building on the other side of Shern Park, on Semple street—fittingly enough—for the Semples to set up another enterprise, to Mary's profit, privately reported by Silas Cole, to replace the Landho tavern. She permitted this one to be named Henry's, as Henry Semple was the best advertisement for what could be found there.

John had the upstairs of the newly renovated tavern building turned into an apartment for himself for the many nights he would have to stay there because of his duties at the tavern. He didn't begrudge being away from home frequently at night—in fact, it somewhat relieved him. Of course to satisfy Mary to this new arrangement, he had to be extra dutiful when he slept at the Geer mansion on the Upper Head. As Mary gave birth twice subsequently, to healthy male babies, the arrangement obviously satisfied her enough too.

73

The one loose end John left—and shouldn't have—was what he had intended to do about his stepson, Garen Fischer. It was a very delicate matter, because Mary doted on her children from her first husband, and John knew he had to walk softly in the world of an established family he had entered. Garen was of age. There was little John could do about the behavior he had seen no matter how disgusted it made him. The problem was so sticky, though, and so unsure was John on how to approach it with Garen—and so busy did he become with reestablishing the tavern as a respectable business—that he eventually let the matter slip his mind.

This was probably a mistake—at least in not having corrected the impression Garen Fischer had gotten by seeing his stepfather enter the tavern and then go upstairs—and, to Garen's knowledge, since he was otherwise occupied, not seeing John quickly come back down the stairs. Garen knew what happened up those stairs. And even though John Dungan was making sweeping changes at the tavern, Garen had no knowledge that John didn't know of the opening of Henry's as a Geer business, and he had no reason to think that John's personal interests were different from what Garen had surmised. In looking in John's glazed eyes that afternoon, Garen had seen what he interpreted as interest rather than shock.

Thus, on one dark night, when John had had such a heavy work day that he could barely climb the stairs to his rooms above the tavern, not to mention the bluff to the Geer mansion on Upper Head, John stripped, doused himself with water from the pitcher on the bureau, toweled himself off, and stretched out on the bed to sleep the sleep of the dead.

So exhausted and deep in sleep was he that the weight of another body coming down on his bed didn't awaken him. Neither did the gliding of a hand over his body or lips on his chest and on his belly and covering his engorging cock. John dreamt of Mary, who, when encountered in the darkness of night was an experienced and inventive lover.

It was long after his cock had been encased by the welcoming, moist warmth of a tight channel and he had encircled his lover with his arms and set his pelvis in motion to meet the rhythm of the hips plastered to him—in fact, at the moment of ejaculation—when he woke up to find . . . that he had fucked his stepson.

Chapter Five: 1995

Driving into the north end of town and turning onto the Upper Head road to rise to the top of the bluff where the three rambling old mansions stood, Eddie Geer wondered why it had taken him so long to visit Shernhaven. He'd always been told that the small, harbor village where his English ancestors had settled in America three hundred and fifty-five years ago was picture perfect and worth a visit. It was less than twenty miles from Boston and he'd traveled the world, but this was his first visit here. The main branch of the Geers had long since moved to Boston, where they had become prosperous in the construction industry and later in the manufacturing of this and that, which they produced just at the right time for consumer interest and then cash in on right before the market on the commodity collapsed.

To be clear, this meant the Geers were among the richest families on the planet.

Descendents of Geers had stayed here for a while after that, but the name had petered out except as it was attached to various businesses in the town and a street he was told ran up from Wharf Street on this side of the central park that he'd planned to locate and take pictures of just for the hell of it—to show around the fraternity when he got back to Cambridge. He half hoped he'd get a photo of a hobo sacked out on a bench or taking a leak in the bushes when he photographed the park.

He wouldn't have come here at all if he hadn't been invited by college fraternity brothers who, as coincidences go, were also from founding families of this little burg and who invited him up here—again just for the hell of it. He wasn't actually all that fond of either Alden Shern or Trevor Cole. Both were pretty full of themselves and about being from wealthy families that were among the early Massachusetts settlers. Who in his Harvard fraternity wasn't from a wealthy family—or even from early American stock somewhere? And the two who were from here were still tied to this hick town. Big fish in a small harbor, and still expecting to get away with that in Cambridge.

Well, Alden wasn't so bad. Dark and brooding. He didn't get snotty when he wasn't around Trevor. It was Trevor Cole—the blond, brick-built, glad-handing, big talker football star—who irritated Eddie the most. Not the least because, despite everything he felt, Eddie felt drawn to Trevor. As a person, of course, there wasn't anything more in it than that. But Trevor was such a self-confident macho dude and had that great build and movie star looks. Everyone bowed down before him. That irritated Eddie too. He was the one with the most successful family coming out of Shernhaven. He was the one with the worldliness. Not much he hadn't tried, although he was running straight now. He'd be inheriting a business that swamped everything in Shernhaven in size and worth. And he was training to take that on.

As Eddie drove past the first house on the bluff, he knew why he'd taken so long to come to Shernhaven. It wasn't just because most of the Geers had moved away. It was about the crazy old Geer woman everyone in the family talked about in hushed tones. She'd been the last real Geer here and had married twice before the Civil War, having wedded "down" both times—once to a German and, worse, later to an Irish Catholic—and had a reputation herself that the Geers twittered about behind their fans in those days.

The plaque in the stone pillar in the wall in front of this first mansion said "Fischer," but Eddie knew this as the Geer house. This was his family's ancestral home, occupied now by peasants, simple fisherman, he'd been told. It was additionally irritating to look at it now to see that the building had been kept up in superb condition. The only satisfaction was in the connection that had been made when Eddie first met Alden and Trevor at Harvard. They had done a double take on his name, and in exchanging family backgrounds, he was pleased to know that although it said "Fischer" on the wall plaque, everyone here still knew the house as the "Geer" place.

Driving on, Eddie passed the next house, which was identified as the home of the Coles on the wall plaque. This would be Trevor Cole's house. Eddie found himself looking at it with great interest—and then looking away with self-disgust. He must break this interest in Trevor Cole, he told himself. There was nothing interesting in the personality of Trevor Cole. It was just in his looks and how he carried himself—and what he had to carry around. The guys had a communal shower room at the frat house. Eddie was breaking away from that now, though. That was all Venice, and he was putting that all in his past. Just experimentation. And he'd rejected it. And he wouldn't have Cole on a Christmas tree. Such an arrogant ass.

He came to his destination, the last house on the bluff, its side toward the sea. The biggest, most imposing one by far. Alden hadn't told him his family was the most prominent one here—and mostly certainly Trevor Cole wouldn't mention it, because it meant his family wasn't at the top of the chart—but the placement and size of this house would have been enough for Eddie to realize that even if the town wasn't named after the Sherns and Alden's daddy wasn't the state senator from this district, Shern was the first family here.

Both Alden's Porsche Boxster and Trevor's BMW convertible were parked in front of the garage doors in a five-bay auto garage to the north of the main residence, away from the side of the head overlooking the town, so Eddie knew they were there already. He was an hour early, so he was relieved that they were there. He'd been told he'd be staying in guest quarters above the garage. So, he parked his Jaguar coupé beside Trevor's BMW and started walking around the garage, looking for the door to the quarters above it.

Strange sounds, almost a deep moan of pain or something, arrested his attention when he'd gotten to the back of the garage building. A small path leading deeper into the trees and brush at the north end of the property drew him forward to where he found a shed. The door was open and the moaning seemed to be coming from there.

As Eddie reached the door, he was shocked at the almost-screamed "Yes!" that exploded out at him from the interior of the shed.

The small room inside was dimly lit, but what was going on there was obvious from the moment Eddie looked inside. It was mesmerizingly shocking. Separate waves of surprise, shock, disgust, and arousal flowed over Eddie all at once, each emotion struggling for ascendance in his senses.

Both young men were naked. The lithe, dark, sinewy body of Alden Shern and the magnificently developed blond-god body of Trevor Cole. Eddie immediately realized that he had suspected something like this, without consciously being aware of it, all along. But it was all wrong. The roles being taken were all wrong.

Trevor Cole was stretched up against the wall opposite to the door, his wrists bound to iron rings high on the wall, his arms stretched and imprisoned. Eddie could barely make out red welts on his back and bulbous buttocks, related no doubt to the whip held in one of Alden's hands. Alden's other hand had just withdrawn from the crease between Trevor's buttocks. The exclamation that Eddie had heard as he approached most likely was linked to being told what Alden was going to do next, because as Eddie stood there, momentarily transfixed, Alden, dressed only in construction boots, took his condomed erection in his hand, pressed his cock up between Trevor's exposed butt cheeks, as Trevor cried out at the initial penetration, and started to fuck Trevor's channel.

Eddie turned and stumbled away from the shed and back to his car. He drove away, down toward the town, where he parked near the town's park, which he scowled to find in pristine condition, and got out and sat on a bench and hyperventilated and tried to calm himself to consider what he'd seen.

The sex—and the nature of it—were shocks in themselves. But the arrangement of it completely blew his mind. Alden was the quiet, brooding, smaller one. It was Trevor Cole who Eddie would have identified as the top in such an arrangement. In fact, it was why he had these mixed reactions to Cole, he now realized. He almost felt nauseous at how wrong he'd gotten it—and at the thought that he might have made a fool out of himself if he'd acted on any of the impulses he'd had in the last year. He bit his lip, wanting to feel the pain, because, shit for bricks, it was still Cole's body that crowded in his mind from seeing the scenario he had just seen. And it still was Cole in a role in his fantasy that was grossly at odds with the reality of what he'd seen.

After an hour, Eddie had pulled himself together enough to decide to drive back up to Upper Head. This was when he'd been expected. It should be fine now. There was no need for him to even hint that he'd been there earlier.

This was actually good. This would help him in his determination to straighten his life out—in every sense of the world. This should even push those memories of the summer in Venice farther back in his mind. But as he walked to the car, all he could think of was Trevor Cole's magnificent body—and what Eddie would like for it to be doing to him. And then the shuddering thought of the sickening revelation that Trevor wanted the same thing from another man that Eddie wanted.

But maybe, just maybe, Eddie thought, not wanting to give his dream up, Trevor went both ways. Eddie could always live on the hope—except, of course, as he kept telling himself, he wouldn't have Trevor as a lover even if that was what Trevor wanted.

* * * *

"Don't you go pouring that beer, son. You know minors can't do that in here. You'll get us shut down."

"Sorry, Dad. Just trying to help, and you look like you need it."

"Needing help at the bar service is cash register joy to my ears, son," Owen Dungan said. "You can help with the serving of the food all you like. And I thank you for coming in this evening."

"I can wash glasses back here, can't I?"

"All the dirty ones you can find, yes." Owen's son went to the end of the bar, and Owen turned to the three college students bellying up to the bar. Despite what he'd said to his son about the underage rules, he wouldn't be asking these three for any

80

identification. Besides he knew exactly how old two of them were. Alden Shern and Trevor Cole he knew very well. Their families owned much of the town and always had. The third young man, looking morose and on edge, Owen didn't know.

If he asked Alden or Trevor their ages, he'd either get back a lie or something he didn't want to hear. He hated having this "nothing good" choice when these guys came into his bar. If this wasn't Shernhaven . . . but it *was* Shernhaven.

When the Shern and Cole boys were in high school, Owen had had to carefully and politely show them the door whenever they walked into Dungan's. He didn't know why they even tried to come here after the first time. As he heard it, they were served beer—and more—at Henry's across the park in those days. They were old enough now, though, for the people who counted in this town to turn a blind eye to their doings.

He served them the beer, but he made a note to keep an eye on the guy who had come in with Alden and Trevor. He looked like a volcano—all calm on the outside, but ready to blow underneath.

Owen had no sooner served the three than he turned to see another young man enter who he'd also have to look the other way in terms of being here and drinking legally. This one didn't bother him doing that so much, though. Wal Fischer wasn't wasting away his time in some fancy-dancy university and wallowing around in his allowance. He was going out on one of his family's fishing boats every day. He was doing the full work of a man, so Owen didn't mind turning a blind eye to his age—he should be able to do the other things a full-grown man could do, as far as Owen was concerned.

Besides, Wal Fischer's family was almost as well established at the Sherns and Coles were in this town. The local law knew how to separate them that had from them that didn't, so Owen could do so as well. Business hadn't been so good lately since other bars had opened around town. They were all in nice, new buildings. Not like this dump that was tumbling around Owen's head but was on the historical register, so there was only so much Owen could do about sprucing it up. Owen wasn't about to turn old-money business away; he had no intention of shooting himself in the foot with the shotgun he had under the counter.

Less than thirty minutes later, he was to regret that thought, though.

It all started with that on-edge guy the Shern and Cole boys had come in with. But no, not really. it had started, surprisingly enough, with Wal Fischer.

Owen always knew there was something not quite right about that boy. He was a solid-bodied, good-looking lad and, as Owen had already contemplated, a hard-working one. But he was always so quiet. Sitting wherever he did and intensely watching without engaging. Watching people come and go—mostly men now that Owen thought about it—coming and going. Owen thought maybe Wal's reticence came from being out on the ocean fishing, alone more often than not. This evening, though, he was being a bit too obvious in his interests.

Alden Shern, Trevor Cole, and the guy with them were at the bar, turned to each other, with Cole in the middle. When Wal Fischer came in, he looked around, and having spied Shern, bellied up to the bar right next to him. The trouble might not have started, except that Wal apparently had a good bit to drink before coming into the bar. He seemed to be just off his fishing boat, and he'd probably gone out that morning with a full cooler of beer cans.

Wal was really close to Alden. The first Owen heard of trouble was Alden calling out a surprised "Hey!" and turning toward Wal.

"I heard you were in town, Al," Wal said. "Haven't seen you since graduation. Since you . . . we . . . well, you know. Missed you. Could we talk a minute. Just a minute. In private."

Alden didn't answer. He didn't have time to. Cole answered for him, raising his voice. "Buzz off . . . faggot. What'yer doing here anyway? Nobody you like hitting on over at Henry's tonight that you like as much as Al? Didn't we take care of you at Shernhaven High?"

Owen saw Wal's hand freeze in midair. It had almost touched Alden's sleeve. His eyes took on a panicked look.

"Now guys. None of this in here," Owen said. And his son put down the glass he was drying and edged down the bar toward his father.

All attention now went to the other guy who had been with Shern and Coles. That volcano erupted right at that point. "Faggot?" he cried out, and he spun around Trevor and Alden, fists flying at Wal. Wal worked his body hard. He could have defended himself against just that one guy without trouble. But he was frozen in shock, so the guy got in two good cuts at his face, before he could get his hands up.

This was when the shotgun came out from underneath the bar.

"I said, none of this in here," Owen said in a steady, determined tone. "Take it out on the street. Outside. All of you."

"Uh, Dad," Owen son said from beside Dungan's elbow. "Maybe not all at once. Maybe Wal should go first and we let the others go after he's had a chance . . ."

"Get the hell out of my bar," Owen said. "All of you. This isn't the place for this—for any of this."

The next morning, When Owen Dungan got the news, he was filled with remorse. His son didn't so much as look at him all afternoon as they were setting up the bar. Relations were too tight between father and son for there to be any bad words, but Owen felt his son's coolness like the admonishment he knew he deserved.

The first thing they heard was that the Fischer boy, Wal, was in the hospital from being beaten badly. It hadn't happened outside Dungan's. It had happened over at Henry's.

As the evening unfolded and patrons came and went in the bar, more of the sordid details came out in dibs and drabs.

Wal Fischer hadn't only been beaten up. He'd been left in the back alley outside of Henry's, naked, with a beer bottle shoved up his ass, and with a sign saying "Faggot" crudely written on a piece of cardboard with a magic marker and stuffed in his mouth.

Everyone knew who had done it—or thought they did. And they were at least partially right. Alden Shern had actually stood pretty much on the sidelines, a little shocked, neither egging it on nor stopping it. Trevor Coles had gotten in his licks, all the time screaming at Wal about Alden being too good for him and that he was already taken. These were the two that the whisperers of the town most identified with the act—but of course these two were untouchable, even though the Fischer family was prominent too, and most people in town liked the Fischers more than they did the other two snooty families living up on the Upper Head.

No one but Owen and his son knew there was a third young man involved. A stranger to them, although the town grapevine being what it was, the Geer name eventually seeped out as well. But at the time Owen wasn't going to say anything, and he made sure his son didn't either.

"We can work on fixing this up later, son."

"Yeah, when, Dad? We shouldn't have let them leave together."

"Yes, I know. But we'll see what we can do later. It's all too volatile now; it will be bad for business to stick our noses into it."

It was Eddie Geer, deeply conflicted and steaming inwardly on what he'd seen earlier that day, who had gone over the top in his explosion at Wal. And it wasn't just because of the altercation in Dungan's. It also was because Wal was a Fischer and was living in the Geer mansion. And was, as Geer repeatedly said at the frat house through the next semester, a "damn Nazi" immigrant who had muscled onto the Geer family tree.

Everything had come together, and Eddie Geer was responsible for reinitiating the attack, the idea to drag Wal to the alley at Henry's, the beer bottle, and the sign.

Wal Fischer recovered. But he didn't really return either to the town or the Geer mansion on Upper Head. He moved to his fishing boat and he did most of the provisioning he needed to do at other seaside villages up and down the coast. He still docked at the Shernhaven wharf. Slips for fishing boats were pure gold by now along the Massachusetts coast. He couldn't give his up or easily acquire another—although in time, he did manage to move it to a slip at a harbor farther south. But after the incident at Dungan's and Henry's, no one saw him put a foot on the Shernhaven dock for some time to come.

84

When Eddie's anger subsided, he was so distraught—not at what he'd done, but at what it told him he still felt about Trevor Cole and the Fischers—that as soon as they reached the Shern house, he got in his Jag and roared down the Upper Head road, turned right onto the Boston road, and never came back.

After watching him leave from the driveway of the Shern house, Alden spoke to Trevor.

"Come inside and let's clean you up."

Alden hadn't participated in the assault, so he was clean. But Trevor was covered with blood—both Wal's and his own.

"No," Trevor growled in a low, thick tone. "I want it. I want it now. Let's go to your dad's shed."

It all had brought Trevor to the boil of a high heat—and his arousal got to Alden too. They were in high, loud fuck in the shed, with Trevor chained to the wall when Alden's father, the state senator, Avery Shern, walked in on them.

Avery was supposed to be in Boston. The state senate was in full session, and when it was he stayed there in the family's Boston residence.

But one of the senators had died early that morning, and the session had been broken for two days in honor of the legislator. Senator Shern had decided to come home for the two nights.

And there he stood, at the door to the specially outfitted shed behind his garage, discovering his son fucking and lashing the bound son if his neighbor.

Most shocking to the senator was that he'd assumed that Alden was safely tucked away at his fraternity at Harvard in Cambridge that night—and the senator had come home because he'd set up a session of his own with one of the Semple men.

Chapter Six: 1996

The July 4th weekend had been a high celebration in the harbor town of Shernhaven since before anyone in the town could remember. And, being a seaside town, celebration here was largely conducted on the water. The whole weekend the harbor itself was packed with pleasure boats from as far south as Martha's Vineyard and north as Gloucester. Only a single channel was kept clear for the movement of vessels in and out of the harbor.

The highlight of the weekend was a Sunday afternoon regatta race of sailing yachts out in the ocean, barely in sight of the Lower Head lighthouse.

By custom, even the fishermen took the day away from their toil. Most of them took their boats out to the regatta course to provide guidance boundaries. Traditionally, the Fischer fishing boats took charge of setting and maintaining the course. They did so again this year, with the exception of one of the brothers, Wal, who eschewed all celebration and took his boat out at dawn as usual to perform his daily troll for cod, haddock, and pollack. In deference to the regatta—and most likely to avoid all contact with those from Shernhaven—Wal had moved his fishing spot more to the south of the approach to Shernhaven than usual.

Wal Fischer hadn't felt like celebrating in this town for nearly a year.

The race got off to a late start because so many yachts were competing in this series of races, determined by craft type, and it took them much longer than anticipated to clear the harbor. But once it started, the regatta went splendidly . . . until near nightfall, when a squall came up from the southeast during the one-man laser craft event.

The boats had been warned of the approaching storm, and the last of the yachts from the previous event had crossed the line, so they all turned toward the harbor. The laser boats were on the course, taking a practice sail, but were being flagged in to harbor because of the approaching storm. Entering the packed harbor for the yachts still at sea was as difficult as sailing out of it had been. Long before the last boat was safely inside the Lower Head spit, the townspeople of Shernhaven could have started at the shipyard and walked all of the way to the south end of the wharf across the vessels in the harbor without touching land or getting their feet wet.

The storm remained mainly out to sea as it swept by, but it had scattered the straggler sailing craft far and wide.

Sitting farther out in the ocean than the race course, Wal Fischer's storm lasted longer than anyone else's. But he'd been in high seas like this before. He rarely let the weather strand him on land when there were fish to catch in the sea, no matter how turbulent. And in recent decades finding fish along the Atlantic coast was getting increasingly difficult. He knew there would be no room for him in the harbor on a day like today, so he just battened down his hatches and rode the storm out.

Within an hour, the storm had cleared and the twilight skies were once more clear.

Fischer's catch had been slight, but he knew that it would be welcome in the fish market at Duxbury, to the south, where there would be a harbor that could accommodate him for the night, so he struck out south. He knew there was no way for him to get to his slip in Shernhaven harbor on this day.

He had barely changed his bearings for Duxbury when the hull of a flipped sailing yacht bobbing in the still-choppy waves hove into sight, and, without a second thought, Wal turned his boat toward it.

Minutes later, he pulled a semiconscious Alden Shern from where he was clinging to a rope lashed across the hull of the flipped laser craft.

Alden was sodden and unresponsive other than a soft moan, and his skin had a bluish tinge to it when Wal hoisted him into his boat. He laid Alden carefully on his back on a square-folded tarp in the waist of the deck behind the deck house, where he'd be protected from the crash of the waves. Wal's immediate reaction was that he needed to get rid of that blue tinge, so he started rubbing Alden's limbs and chest, ripping away his sodden T-shirt and shorts.

Alden moaned louder. But he also gurgled. Wal couldn't tell whether Alden was breathing or not, or if there was water in his lungs. He started mouth-to-mouth artificial respiration. As he continued, Alden was coming to life. And he was coming to life in more ways than one. His body was reacting to the attention it was getting from Wal's rubbing of his limbs and giving him mouth-to-mouth. Alden was getting hard, and, unable to avoid brushing his erection in passing, Wal was getting hard too.

This was what Wal wanted. This was what he'd wanted ever since he and Alden had been in high school together. Trevor Cole had been getting what Wal wanted from Alden. And Trevor Cole wasn't here now.

Wal had fished Alden out of the sea—saved him from peril. Emotions were running high, even Alden's, as he drifted into consciousness, realized he was safe and who had saved him, and was aroused by the massage and mouth work he was getting.

Alden swung an arm around Wal's neck and pulled him close in and the mouth-to-mouth work became a deep, searching kiss. Wal's hand went to Alden's erection and worked it as Alden's groans and moans increased in strength.

When Alden released Wal's lips, Wal looked down into his face with a puppy dog look and whispered a hopeful, "Please."

Alden's answer was to reach between their chests and start undoing the buttons on Wal's slicker. He was too weak still to provide Wal much more than an erection, but at this moment that was all Wal needed. He stripped off his oilskin pants and the sweatpants under those as Alden reached skin through the layers of shirting and twisted Wal's nipples to be rewarded with little yips and grunts and heavy breathing from the fisherman. While still stroking Alden's cock, Wal lowered his face for another lip lock. Alden reached for and grabbed and squeezed Wal's balls and was rewarded by a groan and a deep moan. Wal lifted his leg over Alden's waist, rose on his knees, and grabbed Alden's erection in his fist, positioned his channel over it, and then began to lower himself on the shaft.

He stopped, half skewered, and looked down into Alden's eyes as if to assure himself this was really happening. Alden gave a low, guttural laugh, raised his head to Wal's chest and made Wal cry out and arch his back when Alden bit him on a nipple, following Wal's chest up as it arched. His hands went to Wal's bare buttocks, slapped them hard before digging into them with his fingernails and pulling the globes apart to gain deeper access in Wal's channel for his cock to sink in. He began fucking up into Wal's channel, his cock reaching a new depth with each thrust.

Wild with passion, Wal arched back, grabbed his ankles with his fists, and met thrust for thrust, riding Alden's cock hard and long until both had spouted their satisfaction and were spent.

Wal collapsed on Alden's chest and they both lay there, panting, fighting to regain their breath.

"Sorry," Wal whispered into Alden's chest. "I don't know what happened. I didn't mean . . ."

"You saved my life. And you did mean it."

"I'm sorry. It won't happen again."

"Yes it will. But it will be my way. When I wanted to do it back in high school, you were too scared. If we do it again, it will be my way."

They were silent for several minutes, and when Wal spoke, it was on more practical matters.

"You're still cold. Here, we'll move to the cabin. Towels. You need to dry off. Now I do too. And a blanket. Don't need hypothermia."

Wal helped Alden down to his cabin, which he had made into his home. He was a neat person—and lived a simple life—so the cabin was in order. He pulled the towel off the rack next to his shower cubicle and handed it to Alden as he was lowered to the berth at the far end of the cabin.

"And here's a blanket. I'll just go into the other cabin and get something for you to wear—you're more my younger brother's size than mine. You'd swim in the size I need. Yours are in shreds. Be back in a jiffy."

When he returned, he was holding briefs, a T-shirt, and shorts in one hand. In the other, though, he was holding several lengths of nylon cording and a thin leather belt.

Alden's eyes went to the rope and belt. "You sure? Back in high school—"

"I regretted being scared about what you wanted back then even as you were walking away from me. We can manage here. It's a fishing boat. There are ring handles everywhere in here."

And so there were. There was an iron ring in the center of the ceiling by the berth where Wal was strung up by his wrists. And there were handle grabs on the cabin wall on either side of the berth that Wal's ankles were tied to, suspending him in air, facing the berth nook.

When the welts on Wal's back, buttocks, and thighs were still just pinkish skin from the flicking of the leather belt, Alden stopped and leaned into Wal's back. He was breathing heavy and Wal could feel Alden's larger-than-ever cock throbbing at the small of his back.

Alden moved his mouth to Wal's ear and whispered, "You sure? We could stop here. Just a regular fuck. I'm feeling good enough."

"I want it," Wal murmured. "I wanted it back then. That's what I wanted to tell you at Dungan's last year. I wanted it. I wanted it then; I was just too scared. Oh, shit, yes, I want it."

He yelped and groaned as Alden bit his earlobe before pulling away, and then he was crying out louder. "Oh Damn . . . yes!"

The leather of the belt was digging deeper into his back.

Just when he didn't think his arms and legs could take any more from the weight of the suspension of his body in midair in the cabin, Wal felt Alden's hands at his waist, lifting him, and setting him down on Alden's thighs, now supporting the weight of his own thighs. Alden's hands went to Wal's buttocks. He palmed and spread the globes, and then he was lowering Wal's channel on his super-aroused cock.

Wal's rump nestled in Alden's crotch and his channel deeply skewered on Alden's staff, Alden reached around and took

Wal's own erection in both of his hands. Wal found the edges of the berth nook wall on both sides with the soles and heels of his feet, which he used for leverage to fuck himself on Alden's cock.

With a cry of release—release from all sorts of tensions in his life—Wal ejaculated in three heavy spouts across the coverlet on the boat's berth.

Alden heard the hailing call from beyond the boat's cabin before Wal did. Wal was still hanging, exhausted, his head down, and all of his senses concentrating on the warmth of Alden's cum inside him and the strength with which it had filled him.

One second Alden was there, and the next he wasn't, whispering that he thought he heard something out on deck and was going to go check. And very soon after that, as the voices on deck started to cut into Wal's consciousness, he no longer was alone in the cabin. At first there were two men there, neither one of them Alden. There was the senator, Alden's father, Avery Shern. And there was Trevor Cole. Both looked out-of-control angry.

Trevor stood back, blocking the door. Wal could hear Alden, beyond the door, trying to get back in, but being held back by Trevor.

The senator, Avery Shern, drew near to Wal. Wal heard the man utter something angrily in his ear. He didn't catch it all, just the phrase, "You dare." And then Wal was screaming as the belt buckle lashed at his back and buttocks. He was semiconscious when the beating stopped. Fingers were being run over the cuts and welts that had been caused by the belt buckle. And then the senator, Alden's father, was fucking him from behind, all the time hissing incomprehensible angry words in his ear. Avery ejaculated and then pulled out of Wal's ass—and was gone.

And then there was only one. Trevor Cole, his face red as a beet, a horrific aspect of anger gripping his face, and his hands bunched up in white-knuckled fists.

Wal was helpless, still trussed up, both wrists and ankles bound, naked body suspended in air.

He looked over his shoulder with growing concern and horror, as Cole first picked up sections of nylon cording that were on the deck by the bed and wrapping them around the knuckles of his fists, and then picking up the belt.

Somewhere close to dawn, one of Wal's brothers found his fishing boat, drifting south of Shernhaven, almost to Gumet Point at the entrance of Plymouth harbor leading up to Duxbury. When Wal hadn't returned to Shernhaven harbor that evening or contacted them, which he always did if he was putting into another harbor, they went to two of their other fishing boats and activated the GPS systems connecting all of the boats. This led them directly to Wal, who was still trussed up in his cabin, but beaten almost to a pulp.

He wasn't conscious when they found him, but when they released him and cleaned him up the best they could, being careful of one leg and the opposite arm, both of which seemed to be broken, he came to enough to beg them not to take him back to Shernhaven. Although they pleaded with him to tell them who had done this to him, he refused to answer. He only wanted to be taken anywhere but Shernhaven.

So, they continued on to Duxbury and called ahead for an ambulance to meet them at the dock.

Chapter Seven: May 2010

"Where did you get those? Those look fresh. You said that Cole didn't . . ."

"No, it wasn't Cole. It's OK, it doesn't hurt much."

Tab had called the bank and asked Ben Semple if he was interested in a nooner at the apartment.

"Always," Ben had answered. "I'll be there in ten."

Ben was already stripping his shirt off as he entered his apartment, and that's when Tab had seen the welts on his back.

"God, Ben. They're on your butt and the backs of your thighs too," Tab exclaimed further as Ben stripped completely down. "This was kinky sex. Who did it, if not Cole?"

"It was Avery Shern, OK? Senator Avery Shern. So, it's just going to be OK . . . OK?"

"No, it's not OK. Does he do this often? He fucked you too, didn't he?"

"You asked before. I told you that I sometimes took cock. That's what Shern wants, so that's what Shern gets."

"Here, lay down over here on your belly. Now I know why you have the large bottle of salve that's in your medicine chest. Let me put some more on—"

"I came because you said you wanted to fuck." Ben's voice was defiant, irritated. "I didn't come to discuss my sex life with others."

"And so we will. But why do you let him do this?"

"This is his town. We've been over this before. And he's after my little brother, if you must know. He's barely legal and already Avery Shern is sniffing around him."

"So, you're trying to divert him from your younger brother. You think that's going to work?"

Ben was on his belly on the mat in front of the French windows overlooking the marina, and Tab, naked now himself, was rubbing salve on his thighs and back. Ben sighed.

"No, not if my brother stays here," Ben responded after a moment of contemplation. "But I'm thinking of trying to get my brother away from here. Maybe move him south for college—his grades aren't too good, but he's a fine athlete."

"But he might come back to Shernhaven now and again, right?"

"Right. Oh god that feels good."

Tab had straddled Ben's hips loosely with his knees and was rubbing his hard cock up and down across Ben's hole between his butt cheeks while he was applying more salve to the man's back.

"You really think you're going to keep Avery Shern from a Semple man he wants?"

"I suppose not. But Demonte's barely eighteen. I can keep him away from Shern for a while longer at least. Oh, shit. Oh, holy shit. Shit, shit, shit!"

While rubbing salve on Ben's butt cheeks, Tab had spread them, positioned his cock at Ben's opening, pushed inside, and each of his thrusts was being answered with a "shit" from Ben.

There was no more talking for the next fifteen minutes. Just heavy breathing, moans, and grunts. Tab ran his hand under Ben's belly and pulled him up onto his hands and knees. As Tab fucked Ben doggy style, he ran his hand below Ben's belly and latched onto his cock and jacked him off to a mutual ejaculation.

* * * *

"So, you really are going?"

"Yep, by the time you get off at the bank this evening, I'll be gone."

"I'm going to miss you."

"You don't have to miss me. You could come with me?"

"I don't see how I can. Shernhaven is all I've known."

Tab moved to a more comfortable position, rolling onto his side while rolling Ben Semple with him, maintaining the purchase of his softening cock inside Ben. This placed them both overlooking the masts of sailboats in the Shernhaven harbor marina through the French windows.

"I think that's your problem—why you've said you feel antsy and dissatisfied with so much in life. I think you've been enslaved by Shernhaven and by your boss, Trevor Cole, too. And, even by Avery Shern."

"Well if they could see you fucking me like this, they'd certainly be angry," Ben responded. "Cole knows what Shern does to me now and again—but he can't say anything. It doesn't mean he isn't angry about it."

"I can imagine. I've heard he can be violent."

"Oh, I don't know. I've never seen it."

"That's because you've given him all he wants from you. You've played his slave."

"That's the second time you've used that word. That's a pretty explosive word to use with me."

"And I didn't do it lightly. I think something or someone needs to get your attention. As long as you stay here in Shernhaven, you are going to be a slave to it and to the entitled families who act like they own the town. You don't think that letting Shern chain you to a wall, beat you, and then fuck you is treating you like a slave?"

"My family's been here almost since the founding. We have a street named after us here. How many other black families in Massachusetts can say as much?"

"And all the good it's done you. Your family is respected, yes. Because it knows its place and keeps its place here. You know, sometimes I think our behavior is genetic—that we inherit our proclivities. You said your family operated Hernando's, the gay bar, with its extra services, even before it was Hernando's— when it was named Henry's. Did it offer the same services then?"

"Yeah, I guess so. Some of my brothers and cousins still do that there."

"And they let men fuck them? Your little brother doesn't know about this, isn't likely to fall into this on his own with or without Shern's help?"

"Demonte fucks men. Already. But that doesn't mean I want Shern at him with what he likes to do."

"And this servicing of the white men in this town by Semple cock. How many generations has this been going on? How many generations of Cole men have had their Semple to fuck them? How many Shern men have torture-fucked a Semple?"

Ben didn't respond.

"As I said, sometimes I think it's genetic—that we inherit our turn-ons and our proclivities and positions—in more ways than one—in life. It's a wonder there are so many Semples in the world—or Sherns, and Coles or Fischers, for that matter, from what I've heard. Their men have been so busy fucking each other down through the generation that it's a miracle they had time, effort, and inclination to plow their wives as well."

"As far as Semples go, we've always had enough steam to fuck anything we wanted." Ben followed that up with a low laugh, as if he was taking it all as a joke. But Tab thought—hoped—that he was listening and absorbing. But he'd probed enough.

"But maybe it's mostly environment. We're back to you letting the environment of Shernhaven and its first families control your life. It's you doing the fucking mostly, but even then it's them with a leash around your balls. Who was worried when we started fucking just now that your boss would be angry that you went back to the office late?"

"Well, I don't know."

"Think about it. You know where I'm going next. I'll be there a while. Long enough for you to decide whether you are too comfortable in the subservient role here to break free. And haven't you told me more than once that this loan business is getting to you—that there's no money to give out and that you find it depressing to tell people no all of the time?"

"Well. My area is accounting. It wouldn't have to be in a bank."

"Except that the comfortable place for you is a bank—because the man who controls you is the president of the bank. I said for you to think about it. You could be your own man. You don't have to be the slave element of Shernhaven."

They laid there for several minutes, each listening to the regularizing breathing of the other, the senses of each concentrated on the softening cock inside Ben—until Tab ran his fingers down Ben's belly and took possession of the young black man's cock and began to work it. Each of them knew where this would be going if Ben didn't pull away to return to the bank.

"You've given notice at the shipyard?"

"I don't think I have to. I think by this evening they'll all know."

"I have to get back to the bank."

"I'll bet Cole isn't even there—that he won't be back at the bank for hours yet."

"You think? You just want me to fuck you."

"Yes, I want you to fuck me. Now. It's your turn."

* * * *

"You're late."

"You could have left. You waited for me because you want it bad, don't you? You're panting for it."

Trevor Cole was sitting at the bar in Hernando's, looking quite impatient, two beer bottles on the bar between his hands, one empty, the other getting there.

"You're an arrogant little prick, aren't you?"

"Funny coming from you," Tab responded in an even voice. "You're the one who has been begging me for it. Leaving all those messages at the shipyard. Don't think the guys down there don't know what you are sniffing around for. This is an awfully small town, and you have cut quite a swathe across it. Do you want me to fuck you or not?"

Cole turned redder—but only for a moment. He smiled, although it took him effort to do it and laid a hand on Tab's forearm. Tab looked down at the hand, but he didn't pull away.

"I've got a room upstairs."

"It'll cost you a hundred. For my cock. I don't care what you have to pay for the room."

"Christallmighty, do you have any idea who I am?"

"Yeah, I hear you're a banker. So you have money—at least you do if you want the stud you've been nosing around to get to fuck you. You want to see it first? I guarantee it will make you pee your pants. You don't want to pay, you're wasting my time. I'll be going back to the shipyard to finish my shift."

"OK, OK, here. Here's a hundred."

Watching Trevor pull a few layers off a roll that didn't seem to suffer any for the loss made Tab think he hadn't asked for enough. But a hundred would be impressive for the guys in Hernando's listening in on the conversation as well as they could.

"Barkeep," Tab called out and a big bruiser of a Hispanic man sauntered down from the other end of the bar where he'd been jawing with two good-looking young Hispanic men who were obviously part of crew in here. One of them, clad only in a G-string had just come down from a pole on a raised stage in the back corner of the bar. When the bartender arrived, Tab leaned over the bar and signaled for the bartender to come in close, which he did, and Tab whispered something to him and gave him the hundred dollars Cole had given him.

"What was that about?" Cole asked, as Tab took his arm and pulled him down off the bar stool and pointed him toward the stairs to the rooms above the bar.

"Did you come here to gossip or to fuck?" Tab asked.

"You know, for a hundred bucks you could be a whole lot more pleasant."

"Again, did you come here for a conversation, or for my cock? This is what you paid for." Tab took Cole's hand and laid it on his crotch. Cole shivered with pleasure and said no more as they climbed the stairs.

Then he broke out into a broad grin when they got to one of the small rooms above and Cole turned back toward Tab while stripping his clothes off to find Tab already stripped down to just a red bandana and construction boots.

"How did you . . . ?"

"Andy Stilton worked early summer at the shipyard. As I said, you're pretty much a legend around here."

Tab motioned and Cole sank down to his knees in front of Tab and drew Tab's pelvis toward his face with guiding hands on the young man's buttocks.

"Oh godohogod oh god, I'm gonna come." When they'd moved to the bed, Tab had taken control and was straddling the banker front to back, each sucking the other.

"No you're not," Tab said as he pulled his mouth off Cole's cock and held the other man still on the bed, not letting him twitch a muscle until the rise in the man's juices had subsided.

It wasn't long until Tab had pushed Cole down on his belly and mounted his hips and was plowing him from above.

"Shit! Oh holy shit! I'm gonna . . ."

"No you're not," Tab said, stopping the whole process dead again and holding Cole until he'd stopped writhing and trembling.

"God, you're good. Worth every . . . where? Where are you going?"

Tab had risen off Cole and was moving toward the door into the corridor.

"Where are you going? I haven't . . ."

"And you won't—at least from anything I'll do to you."

Tab had the door open. He motioned to someone out in the corridor, and the young Hispanic who'd been on the pole downstairs slid into the room. Tab pulled the young man to him, both Tab and the young man facing Cole on the bed. Tab embraced the young man from behind and slid his hand down his belly and then on down to cover the mound of the gold lamé G-string pouch. His other hand unsnapped the string at the young man's hip, and the pouch that had been covering the Hispanic's "goods" was replaced by Tab's cupped hand.

"What are you doing? I paid for you. Not for this." Cole's fury nearly choked off his voice.

"It's time you learned that you can't have everything you want, Trevor—that people here know you for what you are. I wouldn't have you for a thousand dollars. And this is what I have to say to your hundred dollars."

Tab virtually carried the young Hispanic to a hard-backed arm chair near the bed, pushed him into the chair, grabbed and spread his legs over the arms, and crouched down and pushed his hard cock up into the young Hispanic's hole. The dreamy-eyed Hispanic cupped Tab's head in his hands and brought Tab's mouth down to his, moaning deeply, as Tab's cock disappeared up into the young man's passage.

When Tab had time to look up from his work, Cole was gone from the room. By then Tab was really into his work and the Hispanic was determined to give him a hundred dollars worth of trade, so Tab moved him to the bed.

Tab needed to work out his anger before he went to his next stop for the day. He needed to be calm and in full control for that. He took out that anger inside the young Hispanic, who yodeled his pleasure as the springs on the bed played a rhythmic symphony of clashing symbols and roaring cum.

* * * *

Tab sat at the bar of Hernando's and nursed a couple of beers for an hour. He rather regretted that he'd only been here that once and now he was leaving town. The Hispanic guy had been a great lay. Tab had intended only to be at him as long as it took Cole to be insulted that his hundred dollars had gone to some other guy's fuck and he'd been left teased but not satisfied. This was something Cole wasn't used to—which was the main reason Tab had done it. The Hispanic youth had earned every dollar, though, and the house pimp sent him hobbling home to recover.

Half past three of the same day Tab pushed away from the bar, acknowledged the wave and blown kiss from another hopeful Hispanic guy dancing the pole, and started off on a sharply uphill walk up Upper Head Road to the Shern mansion at the end of the bluff.

He'd been told where to report in the note his supervisor had handed over to him the previous day. Up until then Tab hadn't known just what day he'd be quitting the shipyard and moving on, but the note had been something he'd been waiting for, so receiving it brought Tab's plans to a head.

100

When the shift supervisor handed Tab the note, he'd winked and told him he was a lucky guy—at least in what he'd be making off the appointment.

"Don't think you'll be up to comin' to work for a few days afterward. But you're covered, it's OK. I recommend you get some Miller's salve before you go up there. And remember who runs this town, in case you might be thinking about makin' waves about it afterward."

Tab didn't ask why he'd need Miller's salve. He already knew. The supervisor seemed a bit preplexed why he didn't ask, but Tab didn't enlighten him.

Tab just grunted and took the note, not being surprised what it said. He'd planned pretty hard to be getting such a note. He'd assessed the situation, let the supervisor fuck him a couple of times, gave him a great lay each time, and then he left it up to the supervisor to pass word up to the top of the bluff to the Shern mansion—which obviously he had done.

Senator Shern's note told Tab where to meet him. Not in the main house but at a shed around behind the five-car garage. Tab was pleased with this. The shed would be more remote than the house. A guy like Senator Avery Shern was sure to have a bunch of servants. But he also probably wouldn't let any of them go near his shed.

The senator was at the shed door, waiting for Tab. They went inside, where Tab saw, as he expected and was counting on, a well-appointed BDSM chamber.

Tab undressed as bidden and then redressed as requested—leather strappings criss-crossing his chest, a leather-pouched G-string, black boots to replace his combat boots, black-leather wrist bands.

Shern expressed disappointment that he had no piercings or tattoos, but Tab just laughed and said he was only into the fuck—that the fuck itself had always been enough for his partners.

Shern rechecked, and Tab confirmed he'd do it any way the senator wanted.

The senator sat on a black wooden throne with spikes coming out of the top of the seat back while Tab knelt between his thighs and sucked him to an ejaculation.

It was after that that Shern's agenda got changed. When he motioned Tab over to the stone wall at the back of the shed and noted that the rings in Tab's wrist bands attached to iron rings on the wall overhead, instead of letting Shern raise his arms and bind his wrists to the wall, Tab pulled off the wristbands, and, after only a cursory struggle in which the senator was overmatched, attached them to Shern's wrists, as the senator hollered and squirmed, and trussed him up to the wall.

Within minutes, Shern's plan to be flogging and fucking a bound Tab had been reversed. Shern obviously was much less accustomed to this role than Tab was, and he'd sworn and screamed and begged in loud tones until he was well past having any dignity or anal virginity to protect. Then he just hung there, whimpering and gurgling as Tab fucked him royally with a flexible rubber truncheon he'd found among Shern's toys. He told Shern that he wasn't worthy of the use of Tab's cock, and he laughed to himself at that little joke. Just a couple of hours earlier he'd been using his cock to fuck an Hispanic male prostitute.

"I have never . . . no one has ever dared . . ." Shern growled in frustration when Tab was done.

"That's why I did it," Tab whispered in his ear. "Now, if you don't want me to look around here for something really, really big to shove up your ass, I want you to tell me something. And I want you to answer truthfully. And if I find out you haven't, I'll be back."

"You'll regret this," Shern hissed.

"Not as much as you will, senator," Tab answered. "Answer my question. Otherwise I'll call the police and tell them where—and how—they can find you."

"What? What? Ask it and go," Shern murmured in an exhausted voice. Shern didn't seem concerned by the mention of the police. And Tab well knew he wouldn't be. The Sherns had had the local police authorities in their pocket before there had been local police authorities.

"Where is your son? Where is Alden Shern?"

Receiving the information he wanted, Tab dressed and moved to the door. Shern cursed him and told him he was a dead man if he didn't release him from where he was bound to the wall. Tab just laughed and walked out of the shed.

He'd been rougher than he'd intended. He'd been rough enough that he was surprised that the old man had taken it. But he wasn't sorry. He probably wouldn't have given it so hard if he hadn't hooked up with Ben earlier in the afternoon and seen what the senator had done to him.

Tab walked back down the Upper Head road, turned right onto Semple and then up to Cushing, where, at the corner Hernando's was located on, he turned left on Cushing and walked across the top of Shern Park to the bus depot at the corner of Cushing and Braintree road.

The bank was across the street from that, and when he looked, Ben Semple was standing in the window of the bank, giving him a forlorn look and a little wave of his hand.

Tab nodded his head, walked into the bus depot, and bought a ticket for Duxbury. While he was waiting for his bus, he went to the pay phone, looked up a number in the telephone book, called the local paper, and told them where they could find Senator Avery Shern, that he probably required finding sooner rather than later, and that they should send someone with an open mind and a keen sense of humor—and with a camera.

He'd said he wouldn't notify the police if Shern answered his question; he hadn't said anything about not notifying the local newspaper.

Chapter Eight: July 2010

"The interview went well?"

"Yes, it did."

"You didn't think it would, did you? You thought Cole would queer it."

Tab and Ben Semple were sitting out on the deck of Tab's waterside cottage overlooking the north end of Plymouth Bay on the estate of the man Tab had found handyman work with and who wanted Tab near enough to visit when his family wouldn't miss him from the big house up on the bluff.

"The manager at the cranberry packaging business doesn't think much of the Shernhaven branch of the Union Bank of Norfolk, so nothing derogatory Cole might say about me would hold much weight with him. And they haven't had an accountant for a while. I think he's pretty desperate to find someone."

"So, you have a decision to make?" said Tab.

"I guess so. Cole has been a real bear recently. He was ragging on me so much, I cut him off of the fucking. I don't think he liked that at all. And I got a summons from Shern too, which I haven't responded to. I got Demonte off to a prep school in Richmond. If he makes the muster there in basketball, they'll find him a scholarship somewhere."

"Asserting your independence more?"

"I've been thinking about what you said about being trapped and enslaved by Shernhaven. Maybe I should try it somewhere else. And the economy's really getting to me. It's tough on a bank loan officer. I don't know how easy it would be for Cole to replace me, though."

"In either of your services for him. Which would be fun to watch in itself, wouldn't it?" Tab could hardly control his smile. This was what he had been after.

"I'd have to find someplace to stay—someplace temporary until I decided this was what I wanted."

"There's plenty of room here, in this cottage. In my bed."

"But the guy up by the big house when we were driving down here—the guy you said you work for and lets you use this cottage. Would he be cool with me being here? You say you're fucking him as part of the bargain. I wouldn't want him to think I was cutting him out. And I couldn't stay here and keep my hands off you."

"I don't think you'd have to. I told him about you—all about you, inches and all—and didn't you see how he was eyeing you when we passed him? As long as you were willing to fuck him too, I'm sure he'd be delighted with the arrangement."

"He didn't look so bad. But how did you find a job with him? What business is he in?"

"I hit the bonanza. I fucked him first. The job came later. Although I'd done some research and he was what I was looking for. They've got a bar like Hernando's down in Plymouth. Keith Dodson was going down there because he has family here and doesn't want them—or anyone else in Duxbury—to know what he likes. I found out that he owned a heating, air conditioning, and lighting business covering the whole region and that there was a lot that a handyman like me could do on that company's calls."

"So, that's a bonanza?"

That stopped Tab momentarily. He was afraid that maybe he'd said too much. But then he smiled and said, "This cottage is the bonanza. The job's good, but I couldn't get something this nice with what I'm paid. Having this cottage as part of the deal is the bonanza."

Dodson indeed was doubly happy at having the big, black beauty Ben Semple staying at the cottage too. So Ben moved in and started working as an accountant for the Duxbury Cranberry Company.

The first weekend Ben was at the cottage, Dodson came down from the big house and Tab and Ben worked him over together. They got him between them, and he found out what DP meant. They thought they'd overdone it from how he was screaming bloody murder—but after they were done he begged them for it again. He probably would have been happy to give them the deed to the cottage after that. He certainly didn't make any waves about having another tenant. And when it later came time for Tab to ask for the use of his motorboat, he didn't even ask Tab what he wanted it for.

On Friday nights Tab and Ben would go into the dock area of Plymouth to Woody's, the bar where Tab had met Dodson. Sometimes Dodson was there and sometimes he wasn't. More often he wasn't, though, because he now had two studs on his own estate to service him whenever he could get away from his family in the big house.

Tab started to encourage Ben to be more independent in his sexual encounters, and he forever was encouraging him to check out—and try out—the talent that came into the bar.

On Saturdays and Sundays when Tab didn't have to go out on a call, though, he liked to go down to the Duxbury fishing docks by himself and socialize with the fisherman, most of whom were out on the ocean every weekday from dawn to dusk.

He let it be known that he'd like to go out and see what fishing was like someday, and more than one of the men with trawlers said they'd be happy to take him out. With Tab's strikingly good looks and honestly work-built body, readiness to give a competent hand, and sandy-haired Irishman's quick smile and friendly quip, he was accepted by the men working the docks quickly and soon was accepted by them even though he didn't go to sea with them.

Among the fisherman Tab got to know and who he'd sit at the Duxbury wharf with at the end of their day on the ocean and his own breaks away from heating, air conditioning, and lighting breakdown calls was one that Tab slowly gravitated to and focused on. Like many of the fishermen, he had the look of northern Europe about him. He was maybe in his mid-to-late thirties with a hard-work-maintained body of a younger man— stocky but solid build, Teutonic-blond hair, a ruddy complexion on a well-chiseled face, and watery-blue eyes that sparkled and a

106

smile that radiated when he was happy. Unlike most of the many men of Massachusetts who were of German descent Tab had met, this fisherman rarely smiled, though. He was often morose, he walked with a pronounced limp, and he was reclusive, living alone on his fishing boat and mixing with others only in the hour of sharing tales of the day and the catch at the wharf-side bar in Duxbury.

It took the longest time for Tab to cultivate his trust and interest. The interest came first, and seemed to be accentuated when Fischer's friends honed in on Tab and Wal shyly withdrew to the background. Tab knew that Wal Fischer was approachable and that he wanted—probably, considering how reclusive he was, really needed—what Tab could give him. Wal couldn't hide his hunger when their eyes met. But he was skittish and had that feel of an empty, defeated man about him.

One day when they were the last to leave the after-work gathering, Tab probed farther into Wal's life than he had when there were more fisherman present.

"You seem to be married forever to your boat, Wal. I never see you socializing around other than with this group here after you return and have consigned your catch. You are a fine figure of a man. I'm surprised you don't party more in the evenings."

"My boat has been good to me," Wal answered after carefully choosing his words. "She's all I need. Certainly all I deserve. And, as far as nightlife, there's really nothing I care for in Duxbury. Talking with the other fishermen after dusk—and you too—is good mixing and about my limit."

"Nothing in Duxbury to please you in the evenings? Have you gone further afield. Maybe your interests are particular. Have you ever been to a place called Woody's in Plymouth, for instance? Or Hernando's up in Shernhaven?"

Wal Fischer froze, as Tab knew he would. It was quite evident that Wal knew what kind of bars Woody's and Hernando's were. Tab felt he had to press the issue with Wal, though. Shock seemed the only way he could do it. He knew what Wal wanted. Tab had to drop the knowledge that Wal could have what he wanted—if he'd be brave enough to give up his self-denial and guilt.

Wal stood, ready to flee. His eyes were blazing and his fists were clinched. Tab didn't think they were clinched to fend him off physically, though, just as a defense mechanism against what Tab was bringing into the light—and perhaps against his own bubbling desires.

"You wouldn't have to go to Plymouth or Shernhaven, Wal," Tab said in a quiet voice. "I know what you want. I can tell from your reactions to me. I am drawn to you, Wal. I can give you what you want. I could be something you care for in Duxbury to please you in the evenings."

What was coming up from deep inside Wal sounded like a death rattle. He gave one bald, pathetically yearning look at Tab and turned away.

"I can be very discrete, Wal. No one else need ever know. Your life and position in Duxbury would not be endangered."

Wal started to walk away.

"Think about it," Tab said to his back. Tab wasn't surprised or distressed at Wal's reaction. It was a hurdle they had to cross, something that needed to be done. He knew that Wal would think of little else until next they met.

Tab wasn't even surprised, although some of the other fishermen were, that Wal didn't show up at the evening gathering the next evening—or the one after that.

The day following that was one of Tab's days off. Before dawn he was down on the dock, standing by Wal's fishing boat and wearing yellow slickers, when Tab came up from his cabin. Upon seeing him there, Wal did a double take and turned to reenter his cabin.

"Wal. You have to go out today. You know you do. And you have to take me with you. You know you do. You know what you want. I have it for you."

"No you don't—I'm sure," Wal said.

"Yes, I do. You like to be dominated. Punished. I can give you what you want."

Wal didn't answer—or look directly at Tab after the first flash of shocked surprise at what Tab had said. But he didn't reenter the cabin. He went about preparing the little trawler for casting off. And when Tab jumped over the gunwale and landed on his feet in the waist of the boat, Wal didn't make any move to throw him off the boat either. He just worked around Tab, who moved to the center of the boat, trying to stay out of Wal's way.

Wal still didn't look at Tab as he maneuvered the boat down Plymouth Bay, around Gumet Point and then northeast, both up the coast toward Boston and out to sea. His hands were trembling on the wheel, though, so, when they were past the buoys at the entrance to the bay, Tab came up behind him and wrapped his arms around the fisherman. He could feel Wal shaking inside his embrace. Tab's hand went to the snaps on Wal's slicker and then the buttons of the flannel shirt under that. He palmed both of Wal's beefy pectorals with his hands.

Tab had been rubbing Wal's puffed up nipples with his thumbs when he felt him shudder and mutter his first low moan. They were standing about a half mile off the land now, pointed north, and Tab could see the Lower Head lighthouse at Shernhaven harbor off in the distance to the northwest. He tweaked Wal's nipples with his thumb and forefinger and Wal gave a little cry, arched his back, and turned his head. Tab took Wal's mouth with his, and Wal's lips opened to him.

So, I was right. That's how it is, Tab thought. He twisted Wal's nipples hard and nipped at his lower lip with his teeth. Wal moaned deeply.

"I can give you what you want. Below. Now," Wal whispered in a hoarse voice. "I'll put the boat to anchor."

Tab had been naked under the yellow slicker jacket and pants and had those off and had turned around before Wal arrived below. Wal let out another moan and sank in front of Tab and took his engorging cock in his mouth.

When Tab was fully erect, he pulled Wal up on his feet and helped him take his gear off.

"Where? The berth? That chair? Across the table?"

"No, please." Wal answered in a hushed voice. "I don't know if you can . . . if you will . . . but, just a minute."

He stumbled over to a bank of drawers built into the forward wall, opened several, and rummaged around in them.

When he turned, he had several lengths of nylon cording and a leather belt in his hands. And he had a pleading, fearful expression on his face.

Ah, Tab thought, The Avery Shern fetishes. Why am I not surprised? But Tab didn't say any of these things.

"Yes, all right, if it's what you want. Where?"

Wal gestured to a metal ring attached to the back center of the berth nook and to two hand holds in the dropped ceiling edge at the front of the berth. These proved perfect for tying Wal's wrists together above his head on the back wall of the berth as he laid on the bed on his back, his legs sticking out over the side of the mattress. The handholds at the front edge of the berth ceiling allowed Tab to raise, spread, and entrap the fisherman's ankles.

The only part Tab didn't like was the beating with the leather belt, but Wal got hard with just a half-hearted flicking at his belly and chest and thighs. It probably had been so long since Wal had had it that mild applications would be all that was needed. Maybe later it would have to be more intense. Tab saw scars that told him that at least one earlier beating had been with the buckle end, but he wasn't about to do that. When he was reaching the edge of what he was willing to do, he stopped and lowered his mouth over Wal's cock and brought him to ejaculation. He resumed the slaps of the belt after that but was relieved when Wal quickly started begging for the fuck.

"Oh shit, oh, yesss. It's been so long," Wal blubbered as Tab worked his cock inside of him. And then Wal was groaning and grunting incoherently as Tab worked the wonders inside him that won him the slobbering worship of any man letting him beyond his sphincter muscle.

After the first time, there was no more beating; Wal was well into the mood. The second time Wal fucked himself on Tab's cock. Tab laid down where Wal had been and Wall was bound by his ankles at rings at the back, lower corners of the berth mattress, with his wrists bound to handholds in the ceiling of the berth nook. Tab held the fisherman steady with his hands on the man's waist as he lowered his channel on Tab's cock and Wal raised and lowered his hips on Tab's staff with the leverage of his feet off the back wall of the berth nook.

Well toward the noon hour, Tab went fishing with his cock again, with the only fish swimming around in Wal's boat being the repeated crop of little sperm wrigglies spewing into the heads of condoms deep inside Wal's channel. Tab could tell that it had been a good long time since Wal had gotten what he wanted.

Wanting him well in thrall to him, Tab fucked Wal four times that afternoon. Both men were in shape and well up to the challenge. Now Wal couldn't get enough of it.

Afterward, after they'd cleaned themselves and while Tab was soothing cream into the slight welts on Wal's thighs and belly and chest, Tab couldn't resist asking about Wal's arousal needs.

"Are the beatings really necessary?"

"To get me hard and wanting the cock. After that, as you can see, not. I can tell you didn't really want to do that. The thought of it—and then the reality of it—always turned me on the most. But I think I may not need much of that anymore. But the binding . . . some form of binding. I don't know. It's always seemed . . ."

"We could try just that. But if it's not more than I did, the belt could . . . just looking at your scarring, though, it looks like you've done much worse."

"Most of that wasn't done for love or arousal," Wal answered in a low voice.

"And the leg."

"As long as we're careful, that won't bother me any, either."

"So, there can be another time?"

"You want there to be another time?"

"Certainly. But I've ruined your catch for the day. There's not much time left today, and you haven't even begun to haul in fish."

"I've already hauled in my biggest catch of the day—and yes, I'll take you out for the day any time you want."

Seven days later, Tab's next weekday off, he was in the cabin of Wal's boat. He was kneeling on the berth, facing the back wall. Wal was spread-eagled on his body, the two attached at Wal's rump and Tab's pelvis. Wal was also facing the back wall of the berth, his arms spread and bound to the ceiling of the berth and his legs spread and bound at the ankles at either end of the front edge of the berth. They had both just come—for the second time, and Tab was running his hands over Wal's belly and chest and kissing the hollow of his neck. Wal's cheeks were still red and there was a trickle of blood at the corner of one nostril from the slaps Tab had had to give him after he was bound to make him hard.

"That was the best," Wal murmured.

"Each time it gets better. Next time maybe no need for any beating," Tab whispered back.

"No. Nothing but the binding and your wondrous cock. Next time."

* * * *

"You want him, don't you?"

"I'm here with you," Ben answered.

"We discussed this a couple of days ago. We're good together, but we're not married, and we won't be. I fuck other guys. You know I do. I don't expect you to be any different."

Tab indeed was starting to cut Ben loose. It was obvious that Ben liked it in Duxbury. His job was working out fine. Keith Dodson even seemed to be showing a preference for black cock, and Tab was fine with that. So was Ben. He hadn't mentioned Cole or Shernhaven in more than a week.

They were sitting at a table at Woody's. The light was dim where they were but brighter over the bar where they were looking. Tab could tell by the way that Ben was eyeing the young guy at the bar that he was quite interested in him. That suited Tab just fine. The guy was young and preppy. He was what Tab would call cute—not very tall, and thinnish—maybe willowy. A pretty face and hair frosted and moussed up in waves on his head. A little effeminate in gestures and eyelash wiggling for Tab, but Tab could clearly see that Ben was hard for him. The hair was an auburn color, with blond highlights. He looked a little self-conscious, like this was his first time in here. And maybe like he was just fantasizing and checking the lifestyle out, maybe even a virgin. Nice touch, Tab thought. He rather thought the lad was laying that on a little thick, but he'd do fine—as long as his name wasn't Cole or Shern.

"No, that's OK," Ben was saying. "He looks sort of lost. Maybe if we see him in here again . . ."

"Looks virginal, untested to you, doesn't he?" Tab said.

"Yeah, sort of like that."

"I'm sort of surprised you like the weak, limp-wristed kind."

"What can I say. It's a fantasy to fuck the lights out of a little piece like that—to hear them squeal at the beginning and then climb and ride the pole when they find how good it feels."

"And you're already fantasizing about sinking your cock in him and listening to him babble—and having him do a pole dance on you."

"Yeah, yeah, I guess so." Ben laughed, but then he raised an arm that met thin air as Tab rose and brushed past him. "Hey, I didn't say . . ."

"You look like you could use some company," Tab said as he saddled up to the bar next to the young guy. The young guy turned and gave Tab an appreciative smile. Tab continued. "What's your name."

"Clem. Clem Stevens. And yours?"

"You can just call me Tab. And, look over to that table over there where my friend's sitting. The big black guy. If you like him, you can call him daddy. He's got a cock that will take your breath away—make you sing like a soprano. You'll be stuffed like you've never been stuffed before."

By the intake of Clem's breath when he looked at Ben Semple, Tab could tell that the young guy liked the looks of Ben just fine.

"He's a Semple. One of the Semples from Shernhaven."

"Oh, god," the twink croaked.

"So you know what to expect."

"Oh, god," young Clem repeated.

"Scared?"

"Yes, of course." But Clem was licking his lips.

"Ever been on a day fishing trip?" Tab asked.

113

* * * *

The four of them went out on Wal Fischer's fishing trawler the next Thursday.

Clem was all nervous talk and flighty hand gestures and attempts at jokes that fell flat but that Tab laughed at anyway as he guided the young guy this way and that on the deck to keep him out of Wal's way as they cast off. Tab made sure he moved the young piece with a hand on his ass and that Ben could see that Clem didn't shirk from this in the least.

Ben was looking nervous too and wasn't saying much. Tab almost laughed had how Ben's shorts were tented and at the "eat you up" looks he was giving Clem, although he was letting Tab do the maneuvering. Tab could tell Ben was on the edge of not being able to control himself. Clem studiously wasn't looking at Ben, which arousing Ben all the more.

Wal was just going about his business until they got out well beyond the land. Then he dropped the anchor and went below into his cabin. Tab followed him after looking around and seeing that Ben and Clem were sitting back on the padded bench at the fantail and had started up a conversation. Ben had a hand on Clem's knee and Clem was gripping one of Ben's biceps and babbling like a nervous idiot, so Tab decided they were on their way to Nirvana.

Wal was stripping down and pulling nylon cording out of a drawer when Tab entered the cabin and shut the door behind him.

"No need for that this time," Tab said. "I come with toys."

Wal looked curiously at what Tab pulled out his pockets. Two intricately fashioned black nylon restraints, a rubber dildo, and a rubber ball mouth gag.

"New position with these," Tab said, holding up the restraints, "and this is because you are going to be so goddamned double fucked that you'd want to be heard back in Duxbury."

The restraints tied Wal's wrists to his ankles, and Wal made quite a bit of noise even with the gag when, crouching between his thighs as Wal laid on his back on the berth, Tab slowly worked the dildo in above his already-entrenched cock.

114

When they were finished and were stretched out together on the berth and cuddling and running their hands over each other's bodies as Wal had discovered he enjoyed, Tab took his game up a notch.

"You ever done a threesome?"

"No. With the black guy out there? With Ben?"

Tab had been amused. He'd wondered if Wal would say anything about knowing Ben Semple when he saw him coming on board. They'd both lived in Shernhaven and were from well-known families there. But Wal hadn't acted like he knew Ben, and Ben, who had been forewarned, didn't say anything either.

"Not necessarily with him, no. Just in general. I doubt whether Ben is much interested in anything we're doing now anyway. Can't you hear the high-pitched screams out there? And, no, I don't really mean Ben later either. Just in general."

"Are you talking DP here? That sort of threesome? Is that was the dildo was about?"

"Not with that, no. With another guy. The three making love all together. The feel of two inside you."

"I don't know."

"But the idea of it sort of turns you on, doesn't it? You can't hide that fattening cock from me. You're aroused by the idea, aren't you? You like to be pressed to the limit. To be punished. You haven't really lost that desire, have you? What would be more taxing then to have two inside you? You handled me and the dildo fine."

A slight pause and then a softly spoken, "Maybe."

"I can tell you're thinking more than maybe. You want me again now. Don't you?"

"Yes."

When Tab came back on deck, he was pleased to see that Ben and Clem were much closer to Nirvana. Both were naked. Ben was sitting on the fantail bench, facing the bow. Clem was in his lap, also facing the bow. Ben's hands were gripping Clem's waist and he was slamming Clem's channel up and down on his cock—and from the rag-doll look of Clem, Tab could tell that Ben had been doing that for some time and intended on continuing to do it for as long as possible.

115

They were way past the screaming-from-the-size-of-him phase, and Clem had the wild-eyed look of never having had it like this before but loving every stroke of it. From where he stood, Tab marveled that such a small opening could swallow such a thick cock. But it did.

As Tab watched, Ben seemed to have broken the thrall of his uncontrolled lust, and he stopped the stroking and embraced the young twink in his arms. Tab heard him murmur an apology and a question on whether it was too much for Clem. But the young man moved his lips to Ben's ear and whispered something Tab couldn't hear. A big smile spread across Ben's face and his hands went to Clem's waist. Immediately he resumed slamming Clem's passage up and down on his cock. Clem began flailing his arms and legs about and squealing like a piglet—a very happy little piglet.

Ah, already at the climbing the pole for joy stage, Tab thought. He was well pleased.

Chapter Nine: August 2010

It was so dark and the waves near the shore were so choppy that Tab had difficulty seeing the little beach on the ocean side of the Lower Head lighthouse, and he almost was at the entrance into the Shernhaven harbor before he got his bearings. He brought the motorboat he'd borrowed from Keith Dodson in to land as close as he dared, dropped the anchor, and slipped over the side of the boat and into the water with his bag of tools hung around his neck.

It was a tiring swim to the little beach below the lighthouse. This was not the sort of exercise Tab was used to. Once there, he rested for a few minutes, took the sneakers out of his bag and put them on, and then carefully worked his way up a steep trail to the top of the head. The path through the rocks had been created by generations of teenagers who kept it discernible by climbing down to the beach at night from the lighthouse to swim, party, and fuck. He'd been lucky none were here now. If he'd seen evidence of a party from the motorboat, he would have had to come back another night. And he was anxious to get this over with.

At the top of the trail, he crouched down in the oat grass and scanned his eyes across the lighthouse compound and then back. A light was on in a second-story window of the lighthouse keeper's cottage that was attached to the base of the lighthouse.

Tab settled down and waited for the light to go out. When it did, he waited another half hour for the lighthouse keeper to have gone to sleep. Then he stole out across the deeply grassed field between the lighthouse base and the cliff verge. This was one of the most dangerous moments, when he was out in the open, the diffused light from the revolving beam at the top of the lighthouse giving an eerie glow to the ground below. The pounding in his ears wasn't only coming from the ocean surf at the base of the cliff.

When he'd made it to the lighthouse door, he quickly used the skeleton key he had that was a master to all of the lighthouses up and down the Massachusetts coast. He had to be quick at this, because if someone had been standing at the window where the light had been on, Tab could clearly be seen at the lighthouse door.

Once inside, he flicked on his flashlight and moved as quickly as he could up the stairs, through the seven stories of circular rooms to the top, where he had to go out on the iron balcony circling the light at its base. Another key got him into the compartment that held the electronics for the light. Tab knew exactly what to do to disarm the light—not immediately, but within a couple of days—so that it would look like normal wear and tear on the components that couldn't be easily fixed by the lighthouse keeper himself—and also so that Tab could maneuver into the position he wanted to be in.

After he'd disarmed the light, sinking the compound into darkness, Tab silently made his way back down the lighthouse staircase and out the door, which he closed and locked from outside so that there was no sign of forced entry—which there hadn't been. Tab had had a key. Then he worked his way back across the tall-grass field and descended the face of the cliff, more slowly than he had come up it, as the night now was pitch black.

As he putted the motorboat back to the marina in Duxbury, keeping the sound of the motor as quiet as possible, Tab contemplated how and when he would make good on his promise of a good fucking for Dodson in exchange for the use of his boat—and for his silence that Tab had borrowed it.

* * * *

"So, you're really going to be moving on?"

"Yes, I don't know when, but maybe soon," Tab answered Ben. "You don't mind, really, do you? You're spending most of your free time with Clem now anyway."

"Do you mind about that?" Ben asked. He and Tab were both sitting on the deck of the seaside cottage, eating their lunches out of fast-food restaurant sacks, on their lunch breaks from their separate jobs. Tab was right. These lunches where they'd both had the urge to eat at home rather than on the job were the largest blocks of time of seeing each other in the past couple of weeks. Ben had fallen head over heels for his sweet little guy. Clem responded to Ben's fucking as if each was the first time anyone had debauched him, and Ben found that a real turn on. And as far as he could figure out, Clem was the first lover he'd picked out for himself. Tab hadn't counted. Tab had picked Ben out after Trevor Cole had sent him after Tab. Everyone else in his life had either begged him for it—because he was one of the Semple studs with muscles and a big, black cock—or had demanded it from him, as by right.

"No, of course not. We've discussed this before. I'm glad you found him." Tab smiled when he used the word "found," but he was careful to turn away from Ben. Found him in a rat's eye. Tab had found Clem and put the two together. He'd fucked Clem himself before he'd introduced him to Ben and found him quite the tease and delight. Quite a good little actor that, Clem was. A talent for making the other think he was the first, the only, and the best. But Tab didn't think it was all acting when it came to Ben. Clem had acknowledged to Tab that he melted for big, black cock, and thus far it did appear that he had melted for Ben.

But Ben had been Tab's chief concern. He had figured that Clem would be the exotic little tail that would be just right for Ben—a great actor and able to make Ben marvel each time he was able to get his entire cock stuffed in that seemingly small hole— and Tab had proved to be right. Clem was just the consolation Ben needed for Tab to move on. Tab didn't want Ben to get hurt. In all of this, he didn't want Ben to come out a loser. And Tab hadn't been lying when he said he thought Ben needed to be clear of Shernhaven and Trevor Cole. Although he'd used Ben, Tab didn't regret what he'd done. At the same time, he wanted this element of what he was doing to be fixed right.

"Clem wants us to live together. I'll need to be looking for another place."

119

"I don't see why," Tab answered. "As long as you're willing to give Keith Dodson a fuck every once in a while, I don't see why you don't just take over here. Have Clem move in here with you. It isn't much of a drive to that hair salon where he works. I think you should continue to fuck other men, though. I think that will keep Clem in line. He's so highly strung, I think you'd do well to keep him in his place. When he gets snotty, just deny him the cock. He'll come crawling back for it. I've watched him. He can't get enough of you."

"Thanks. Maybe I'll take you up on that. Guess that means you really are serious about moving on."

"Yep."

"You've been hooking up with that fisherman, Wal Fischer. You going to just up and leave him too?"

"I like him. I'll probably keep in touch."

"That would be good. I've always liked him too. He got a raw deal back in Shernhaven a long time ago. A lot of us felt bad about that. I'd hate to see him get hurt again."

"I sensed that when we first met—that he'd been hurt before. I've been working on helping him get past that. I won't just fuck him and walk out on him."

"That's good to hear. And Keith Dodson. Have you told him yet that you're pulling up stakes? You work for him. He relies on you more than just for a fuck when he can get away."

"I don't feel much responsibility for Dodson. He's getting what he wants through deceit of those who have committed to him. And, no, I haven't told him I'll be quitting. I'll either tell him when I'm ready to leave or you can tell him later. He won't get angry with you if you've got your cock inside him when you tell him and if you tell him I didn't give you any warning either. I'm looking for one more special job and then I can cut out of there."

"One more special job?"

"Yeah. There's something special I'd like to fix. Just waiting for the call."

"Is that why you've been glued to the office the last couple of days and calling in every hour to ask what they've got going?"

"Yeah, I guess so."

"You are quite a fix-it man, aren't you? You've got something up your sleeve."

"I've got something up my pants too that could use a little attention. I got thirty more minutes before I need to be back. How about you?"

"I think I can manage that," Ben said as he heaved himself out of the Adirondack chair he was sitting in and opened the screen door to the cottage's kitchen.

"We'll see from your screaming how well you manage what I've got for you up my pants," Tab answered with a laugh, as he too unfolded from a deck chair and turned toward the house.

Tab got back to his office just in time to be there when the call came in.

"It's the keeper at the Lower Head lighthouse," the dispatcher, Cindy, called out to Keith Dodson, sitting in his office and dreamily watching Tab standing at the dispatcher's counter and leaning on it with both elbows. "The light's out for some reason. He says he needs someone out there today to try to get it fixed before dusk."

"I'll take that job," Tab called out to Keith. "I've always wanted to see what those old lighthouses were like."

He smiled to himself as he walked out to his truck. It had worked like a charm. When he had told Ben weeks earlier that landing his job with this heating, air conditioning, and lighting firm had been a bonanza, he hadn't really been talking about getting a cottage beside the water with the deal. What he'd been talking about was finding out that the company had the government contract for electronics maintenance of all of the lighthouses up and down the coast of Massachusetts.

Tab had come to Duxbury for one reason but had found that he had help here to work on the next problem after the one in Duxbury was in hand. He'd known before he got to Duxbury that the next stop would be the Lower Head lighthouse.

* * * *

"It's the light. It doesn't work. I looked in the electronics box, but I can't see anything wrong."

121

"Let's have a look at it then," Tab said, giving the lighthouse keeper a winning smile. The man was rather short with dark hair—a sensual, brooding aspect altogether. He was a good six or seven years older than Tab was, maybe mid thirties. And he had kept himself in good shape. He was relatively small compared to Tab, however—but everything was in perfect proportion.

It was so desolate up here on the Lower Head, the lighthouse compound providing the only structures on the whole ridge arcing out around the Shernhaven harbor, Tab surmised, that working out was probably his main activity. There wasn't much to do at a lighthouse as long as everything was working right. Whatever the case, the guy had kept himself in top-notch condition.

Having the light break down was about the only reason to have anyone else coming up here.

"Why don't you come on up with me? I know I can hardly miss finding it as long as I go up, but I might need some help—and I'd appreciate the company."

Tab looked at the other man hard. The guy was eyeing Tab almost hungrily, trying to hide it, but Tab was a pro at this. He could always tell when a man was interested. He'd worn a tight T-shirt and tight shorts with no underwear—and construction boots. He knew he looked good. He knew that the material was pulled tightly across his butt. And he knew that the line of his cock could be seen inside his trousers from where the man was standing.

He chatted amicably with the man as they walked up the seven flights, Tab making sure he got ahead of the other guy so that his nose would practically be in Tab's butt crack as they went up the narrow, steep stairs. Tab asked him a few things about the lighthouse and what was in the circular rooms they went through and what the equipment lying around did, but he was careful to keep the conversation shallow and not to chatter too much. He knew the guy would not be having much outside contact. All Tab wanted to do was to establish a comfort level—and to start weaving an atmosphere of sensuality with his voice. He knew he was good at that. He wanted to sell himself—his body.

"Here. I think I see what your problem is," Tab said as they were standing, close together, looking into the electronics box just under the light. "Come look in here so you can see the unit I'm talking about."

The man came in close and Tab laid a hand on his shoulder, knowing that it would cause the man to shudder—which it did.

"I tell you what. I'll talk you through taking that unit out, and then we'll replace it with another one. I've got one here in my bag. If it's what went wrong, you'll then know what to take out and how to get a replacement in. I can leave another unit—I have more in the truck—and then the next time it goes out, you can try fixing it yourself before needing to call us in."

"OK. In like this? That doohickey back there?"

They were standing rubbing up against each other, both trying to be directly in front of the opening of the electronics box. The man's voice had been low, hoarse, clogged with what Tab knew was arousal. Tab's hand had dropped to the small of the man's back, right above his rump. Tab could sense the man's buttocks twitching, wanting Tab's hand to move down. The man was fighting against his instincts—just as Tab had planned.

"There. That isn't hard, is it?" Tab said, pulling away and giving the man a big smile. "I'll get another unit from the truck when we get downstairs. I'll have to stick around for a couple of hours, though. We'll need to put the light through its paces to ensure that it's been fixed. I'll sit out in the truck."

"Uh. No, you don't need to do that. Come on into the cottage and I'll fix us a couple of beers. You can drink while you're on the clock, can't you? There's no one else up here on the head to object—or even to know you did it."

"Ummm, that's right neighborly of you. I'll have to change shirts while I'm at the truck, though. I got grease on this one—and on my hands. I wouldn't want to be trucking that into your house."

Tab stood at the driver's door of the truck and slowly peeled the T-shirt over his head. He made quite a display of doing that—and of flexing the muscles that appeared from underneath it. It wasn't the muscle flexing that would do the trick, though, he didn't think. For the last couple of nights, he'd been beating himself—his back and his chest—with a small horse whip. Just enough to show welts. This is what Tab was counting on to push this guy over the edge.

He was displaying himself on purpose. He languidly wiped the grease from his hands onto the T-shirt. He pulled another T from in back of the driver's seat, but he didn't pull it on. When he turned toward the doorway of the cottage, where he knew the man had been standing, taking it all in, he only was wearing the shorts and the construction boots. The shorts barely tickled his hips, showing the line of his flat belly and curve below the plate of his abs. It also dipped enough in front to show the curling of the upper reaches of his pubic hair.

The other man's facial expression showed that he was steaming hot—and it wasn't from the temperature. Tab's efforts of being close to him at the top of the lighthouse hadn't only worked on the man either. Tab was half hard, which could clearly be seen through the tight material of his shorts.

He walked slowly toward the cottage door and tucked the T-shirt in the waistband of the shorts to one side.

The first floor of the cottage was essentially one room, with a counter dividing the kitchen area from the living and dining areas. The man motioned Tab to sit at the dining table while he went to the refrigerator in the kitchen for the beers, but Tab perched on a bar stool at the counter instead.

The man turned and handed a beer to Tab over the counter and then came around the counter and sat at the dining table. Tab swiveled back on the stool, his legs spread, and his elbows back on the counter. His muscles were stretched and there was a line of hard, naked flesh from his throat down to an inch of pubic hair below his belly. The crotch of his shorts were as tented out as the tight material would permit.

"You live alone up here?"

"Yes."

"How long?"

"Almost four years now."

"It must be lonely up here. Do you get down into Shernhaven much?"

"I like the solitude. That's why I'm up here. To forget. And, no, when I come down off the head for provisions, I go into Beechwood, not Shernhaven."

"Shernhaven's a bigger town. More going on there."

"Yes, precisely."

"Must have been something really bad happened in your life to want to isolate yourself like this. What do you do for fun?"

The man's hands were trembling so bad, he was holding the beer can with both hands. Still he was having trouble finding his mouth with it. His eyes were plastered to Tab's naked torso. From what Tab had learned, he had to believe that the sight of the welts was unhinging this guy.

"I've come up here to get away from the fun. Let's just say I've had my fun and it led to something I'm not at all proud of."

Tab ran a hand down his belly. When it reached the fly of his shorts, he unbuttoned the top two buttons.

"Was it sex?"

"Yes," the man answered. He tried looking away, but he couldn't manage it for more than a couple of seconds.

"With a man?"

There was no verbal answer—just the sound of jagged breathing as the man gasped.

"I'll bet it was with a man. You're sexy. I've got built-in radar. I know when there's a man around who could treat me right. And I'll bet you're a top. I'd like that. And I bet you can punish a man. I like a man who can really make me feel it."

Tab ran his fingers along one of the welts on his torso, and he was rewarded by a low moan from the other man.

"You can't deny having your fun for the rest of your life— not just for whatever you think you've done before. You can always start again. You're too sexy to not get back on that wagon."

The bottom two buttons of Tab's shorts were opened, and his half-hard cock spilled out on its own.

"Nobody up here but just you and me," Tab said in a low, hoarse voice. "You said so yourself. No one to object or even to know. I've been horny for you since I drove up and saw you walk out of your door. You gonna make me beg? Or aren't you a top as

I thought? Maybe you're not man enough to make another man feel it."

Giving out almost a primeval growl in the back of his throat, the man was across the room. He had his hands on Tab's chest, his trembling fingers tracing the welt marks Tab had inflicted on himself. And then h was kneeling between Tab's spread thighs. Tab cupped his head in his hand, helping to guide it bobbing back and forth.

"Oh, yes, daddy. Such a sweet mouth. Oh yes, treat me right. You got a bedroom upstairs? You got something that will make me feel it?"

When they got upstairs, Tab came up with two pairs of plastic wrist cuffs. He looked over at the brass bed. "The rails on that headboard strong?" he asked. "Springs good? Won't give in? I have quite a thrust when I'm fucked."

"I swore. Never again," a now naked man muttered. "That's what got . . ."

"But you want me bound, don't you? Was I wrong in seeing that in you?"

"Oh, god," the man whispered.

"I want to feel it," Tab murmured. He didn't, really, but he had read what might be needed to gain complete control. And he had steeled himself to the need.

"I don't have—"

"My belt. Not much. but to get me harder . . . Oh, shit, yes . . . Daddy. Yes!"

The man fucked Tab with his wrists bound over his head at the brass headboard, but Tab was just as happy that the man had given up any more brutal fetishes he might have had at one time than just a few flicks of the belt. Maybe the binding was enough for what Tab had in mind.

They fucked twice—once like animals, reflecting how long the man had been holding himself back—and the second time languidly, as if they were seasoned lovers. Tab didn't need his hands to coax a lover to be enthralled with fucking him. Tab had a talented, well-trained channel, the muscles of which were trained to draw a dick in and undulate the muscles of the channel's walls over it until man felt like he'd never been as hard, had never filled another man like that before, and had never spouted that much ejaculate.

Freed after the second coming, Tab and the man embraced like they were one breathing unit as they stretched out on the man's bed.

"I guess we should know each other. We didn't exchange names when I arrived. I'm Tab."

"I'm Alden. Alden Shern," the man whispered back.

Yes, yes, I know, Tab thought to himself. But what he said was, "Of the Sherns of Shernhaven?"

"Yes."

"And you are up here—secluded—because of something—"

"Yes, years ago, I caused great pain to someone—twice. Not just physical pain. Not like you said you like. Someone I might have loved but didn't give a chance. My father . . . I can't really say what he did . . . but I didn't want to use people as he did . . . to get my way and push others around. I didn't want to be like him. I withdrew here, trying not to be like him."

"And it's hard, isn't it?"

"Yes."

"Sometimes I think it's in the blood. That generations and generations of people just repeat what they do over and over again. But I think it can be controlled and channeled too. And I don't think that being alone up here is the answer."

"It was my choice. And I am alone up here."

"You don't have to be."

"What do you mean?"

"I can get someone to come get my truck. I can live here, right here in your bed, sustained by your cock inside me—at least until you decide you want to live again."

Alden's response was to take one of Tab's wrists and bind it to the headboard again with one of the plastic cuffs—and then to reach for the other willing hand.

Late in the night, as they laid in each other arms and watched the revolving of the lighthouse beam above them through the open window, Tab whispered in Alden's ear.

"The two of us. It's wonderful. Ever thought about doing a threesome, though? Ever wondered what it felted like to have your cock rubbing against another guy's inside someone else?"

Chapter Ten: September 2010

"I shoulda gone out to do the fishin' today. It's a great fishin' day."

"You fished Sunday to free up today—and you brought in a big catch that day."

"I don't think this is a good idea."

"You've been thinking this was a good idea for a couple of weeks. You couldn't help but show your interest when I mentioned it. I bet you've been hard ever since."

"I don't like comin' in to Shernhaven harbor. I said I'd never—"

"You're doing a lot of things you didn't think you'd ever do again—and you're having a ball being balled."

Wal Fischer turned and looked Tab full in the face.

"I don't like bein' pushed like this."

"Yes, you do. Being bound to the plow makes you melt. If I beat you into submission to come here today, you'd love every stroke of it. Pull on into the harbor. I know you're stalling. I promise we won't be in the town long. As fast as we can walk across it, we'll be out of it."

"I'm not sure about this threesome thing."

"And that's why you've been hard for a week just thinking about it? You are as curious as the next guy. But if you find you don't like it, we'll leave and not come back."

"I'll probably be tied up."

"I'll untie you any time you want. You've got to trust someone. There's no reason why it wouldn't be me. I'm not any part of anything that's messed around with you."

"I don't think I can take—"

"Yes you can. Another cock is more flexible than a dildo. You loved it."

Tab tried to say he wasn't messing around with Wal with a straight face. If he hadn't been part of what messed Wal Fischer up, he wouldn't need to be here.

"Why are we goin' into Shernhaven harbor if we're not gonna be in the town."

"We're going up there, if you must know—to the Lower Head lighthouse." Tab pointed up the ridge they were gliding past, to the lighthouse. "If you know of another place to put this trawler in that we can walk up there from—not take a taxi or anything, since you won't want folks to know you're here—then you tell me how we can get there. You've got a slip reserved at the southern end of the wharf at Shernhaven. We can climb up to the top of the ridge from there. There won't be another building we'll have to pass between there and the lighthouse."

"I don't know. Isolated out there like that. I've never been to the lighthouse."

"Sure you have—at least beside it. Don't tell me you didn't go to the beach below that for fuck parties."

"I wasn't much for fuckin' then. The one I wanted to fuck me wouldn't."

"The isolation is part of the charm of this little rendezvous," Tab said, moving the conversation away from a bitter past, not wanting to get to close to what underpinned all of this. "You're a screamer if we don't use the gag—especially when you're doubled. You can scream in ecstasy all you want up at the lighthouse. The wind will carry it out to sea."

Wal turned and looked sharply at Tab. But then he couldn't help himself. He laughed. That took the tension out of the air, and he efficiently, without wasting time, motored around the Lower Head spit and into the Shernhaven harbor and headed toward the Fischer company slips at the south end of Wharf Street.

Few words were spoken thereafter as the two huffed up to the Lower Head ridge in the early afternoon sun. There was a slight nip in the air and the breeze was blowing out to sea.

130

"There," Tab said. "Any noise we make goes out to sea, not into Shernhaven. They won't even know we've ever been here."

Tab pushed a still-reluctant Wal along. Tab wanted this to work, the first time. He didn't want to have to figure out how to do this again. He had wanted to be back south again before the cold weather set in in Massachusetts. He hoped he'd be able to do that, but Wal's reluctance wasn't making him feel real confident about that. In just a few minutes, he'd know whether it would work or all blow up in his face. He'd figured that if Wal was prepared for even more than he'd get, there would be more of a chance of the plan working. Tab certainly hoped that was the case.

Few words were spoken either when they got to the lighthouse cottage door. Tab stepped up to the door and knocked. And then he held his breath and gave a little prayer.

Two surprised exclamations ensued when the door opened.

"Wal!"

"Alden!"

It had been a chore, but Alden Shern and Wal Fischer once more were within arm's reach of each other.

Upstairs the two other men shyly looked at each other—wanting to say something, but not being able to find the words, their eyes and bodies answering for them as they both stripped down and saw each other again—both still hard-bodied after fourteen years—both, judging by the hardness of their cocks, able to arouse the other.

Alden walked over to Wal and gently traced the aging marks of the belt buckle on Wal's chest. There were tears in his eyes.

Tab, already quickly naked himself, was pulling toys out of a duffel bag he had carried up from the fishing trawler. He turned to the men.

"Your choice, Wal."

In one hand, he held out the wrist-ankle cuffs he'd regularly used with Wal on his boat and the plastic cuffs he and Alden had been using here, in this room, on the headboard of the

131

brass bed. In the other he held a riding crop, a rubber dildo, and a ball gag.

"If you aren't worried about the noise carrying down to the town, Wal, we'll dispense with the gag. I think Alden will want to hear your response to him after all these years—I know I will. And we might not need the dildo or the riding crop, either. I don't think we'll need a dildo when a second natural cock is available."

Wal shivered and let out a little moan. Alden, not briefed beforehand but fully in the moment, moved behind him and encircled his waist with his arms and, after kissing the old scars on Wal's shoulder blades, buried his lips in the hollow of Wal's neck.

"We're both going to fuck you, Wal. Together and at the same time. Gag or no gag? How strong is that bed of yours, Alden?"

It was all show. Tab knew full well what punishment the springs of that bed would take.

Wal moaned deeply again. Tab knew that moan. Wal was going to have a good time. He'd be mighty glad he'd come. Tab laughed at the thought—and come and come and come again.

The doubling was just a threat—to cause Wal's mood to spill over. Both Tab and Alden did work him together, and both of them did fuck him when the three were entwined with the others. But Tab fucked him first. And then, when Alden took over the honors, Tab slowly worked his way out of the threesome and off the bed, After cleaning himself up in the bathroom, he slipped out of the cottage, carrying his somewhat lighter duffel bag, for the solitary walk back down to Shernhaven. The last he saw of them, Wal was bound by his wrists to the rails of the brass headboard and Alden was pounding his ass like there was no tomorrow. They hadn't used the riding crop or the dildo. And neither Wal nor Alden seemed to notice that Tab was gone.

* * * *

Tab spied the young guy from across the bus depot waiting room. He got up and sauntered over to the stand where they were selling newspapers, magazines, and candy. The young man's eyes followed him. He looked familiar. Maybe a younger version of one of the guys Tab had worked with at the Shernhaven Shipyard. Andy Shelton his name was. Could be a younger brother. Not a football player, though. More a swimmer. A lithe, flexible body. Tab could tell that by the way he'd moved when he'd come into the waiting room. Yeah, Tab would like a piece of that.

And from what he could see in the rigidity in the young man's body now, as he surreptitiously eyed Tab, Tab could tell that the guy needed to have someone get a piece of him. Tab had seen this before—mainly with young men unsure of themselves and guilt ridden but wanting it, needing it if they were ever going to be comfortable in their bodies. And this one had a very nice body indeed. Yep, Tab thought, what this young guy needs is to get laid. He needs a handyman. He needs to be fixed.

* * * *

Tab had walked down from the lighthouse, along the ridge of the Lower Head. All the time he walked, he was looking down into the town. Probably for the last time, he thought. It certainly looked like a nice town on the surface. Surface looks could be deceiving, though.

He was carrying his duffle bag. He'd left the sex toys behind, but he had the other clothes he'd come to Shernhaven with a few months previously. He'd just leave with what he'd brought. He wouldn't take anything else away from Shernhaven. There wasn't anything else he wanted from Shernhaven ever again.

When he got to Shern Park, he walked west on South Braintree Road to where the bus depot was on the corner of Braintree and Cushing. He took a look at the bank building across the road from the bus station. Trevor Cole was standing in the window. When he saw Tab approaching, he abruptly turned and disappeared into the shadows.

Tab bought his ticket and settled in for a two-hour wait. The bus that would head down to New York, on to Philadelphia, and then down the seaboard on I-95 would leave at twilight. Tab was going farther south than Philadelphia—to where there wasn't a nip in the air already in September. It would be night beyond New York. It was while he was sitting there, waiting, thinking about what had happened here over the past few months, that he saw the young man walk into the depot and over to the ticket counter.

When it was time to board, Tab held back. There were only four of them boarding the bus. When he mounted the stairs, he was happy to see that the old man and woman were together and were sitting near the front. The young man had gone to nearly the back of the bus. Tab walked down the aisle, his eyes on the young man's face the whole time. The young guy couldn't hold his eyes; he looked away.

But Tab knew. The guy had picked a seat near the back and moved to the window seat. He probably wasn't figuring on anything actually happening. He was just fantasizing, too up tight and scared to go farther with anyone. But he was in for a surprise.

There was a look of surprise but also a little smile on the guy's face when Tab sat down in the aisle seat beside him.

Tab felt the young man trembling. He knew he was half way there.

"Going far?" he asked the young man as the bus started up. Tab looked across him and out of the window. Trevor Cole was standing out on the sidewalk outside his bank, giving the bus a hard look.

"Philadelphia. Back to school. You?" He had to clear his throat as he spoke.

"Further south. Back to the sunshine. You from Shernhaven?"

"Yeah. All my life. But I feel freer the longer I'm traveling away from it. That's why I applied to Temple. Gotta get out of this town."

"Wise decision."

"And you?"

"Just drifting through . . . this time. So you're a student. A college student?"

"Yeah, I'm a sophomore."

Good to know, Tab thought. Free game. Past time when he should have accepted it.

"And an athlete too, I'd guess. Good body. Really good body. You're wise to keep yourself in shape like that."

"Track. The hundred-yard dash is my specialty, but I'm trying to work my way into pole vaulting." The guy was obviously pleased, but he sort of shrank in upon himself in response to Tab's comment on his body. He couldn't withdraw into himself enough for it not still to be obvious that he had a well-worked body, though.

Not a swimmer, but close, Tab thought. And he does need to work his way into pole vaulting. I've got a pole for him to vault.

"And you? What do you do?" The young man had spoken shyly, like he was on edge on deciding whether he wanted to continue the conversation. Tab assumed he did want that—and more—but that he was tottering there on the edge, scared of going over the edge. Tab wondered what experience he had, if any. Surely he'd known why Tab came back and sat next to him rather than in any of the other many empty seats on the bus. And whether or not he would consciously admit it, his own fantasies were what led him to pick a solitary seat at the back of the bus in the first place. He had invited it.

"I'm just a handyman."

"Ah, a Mr. Fix-it. Fixed much while you were in Shernhaven?"

"I hope so—at least for now, I hope. But fixing things isn't forever. Things seem to be what they want to be. You fix them, and then you look around and they're broke again."

"Sounds like Shernhaven. The more things change and get fixed, the more they go back to the way they were."

"Yes. Exactly. What's your name."

"Sandy."

"Sandy what?"

"Just Sandy's enough."

That's when Tab was sure. The guy wanted it. He was scared of getting it, but he wanted it. All that was needed was to play him right and then he'd open right up. Tab bet he would be a great fuck, that he'd be burbling his thanks after he'd finally given it up. Maybe not so good if he was a screamer, on the bus like this. But even if so, Tab had that red bandana in his duffel. They could

135

use that. Tight. If he was new to it, he'd be tight. Tab liked that thought.

If he'd given his last name, Tab wouldn't have been sure, despite all of the body language. But he didn't want to give his name. He was hoping for action on the bus—if only the possibility of something he could fantasize about later, when he was alone. The exotic nature of having or even fantasizing sex on a bus, especially when all you've managed to do about having sex with a man before was in your dreams of exotic locales. Buses weren't that exotic for Tab, though. This was a favorite place to have sex for Tab. A fresh, tight ass, though . . . that was something even more a favorite.

"As we were saying, there seems to be a lot going on under the surface in Shernhaven," Tab went on. "Some would say it has a seamy underbelly."

"Yeah, that's the truth. You must have been pretty long to see that."

"Long enough. Sort of an interesting thing going on under the surface, though, don't you think? A man could really be free to rock out in Shernhaven. He could really come in touch with who he really is, don't you think?"

"Don't think much about it. There are a lot of expectations of what a guy is supposed to be and do. I try to focus on my sports. I think that's going to get me to where I'm going." The guy was getting nervous now. It was becoming more evident that they were talking about the same thing.

"Yeah, sports are good. There's a lot to be experienced in life, though, don't you think, Sandy?"

"Well . . ."

"Ever been to a bar in Shernhaven called Hernando's?"

Sandy froze. When he answered there was a shake in his voice. "No, of course not. I'm only nineteen and it's a bar and . . . well . . ."

"You know you can't wish away your feelings, Sandy. If you go through life just being what you think you're expected to be and not living life to the fullest of your desires, you will have missed out on a lot in life."

"I pretty well have my life mapped out for me if I keep clean and study and practice hard. Temple's a good feeder school for Penn State for athletes. I do well with the grades and the field competitions there and—"

"Why do you think your eyes were following me around in the bus depot, Sandy? Why do you think you came to the back of the bus, where no one else was, to sit? Your body knows. Listen to your body. Hell, look at it. Look at your crotch. You're hard. You're hard for me. You want it. You've wanted it for some time. You've just been too scared to step over that line." Tab was keeping his voice low. But he knew that Sandy had heard every word. He had taken each one like a body blow, each one knocking one more brick out of his defensive wall.

Sandy could hardly speak. He went rigid and when he did speak, it came out in a raspy croak. "Shit, man. I didn't mean . . . hey. What'yer doing? Stop that, I—"

"I don't think so. I don't think I'm wrong. Tell me I'm wrong."

Tab already had Sandy's fly unzipped. He reached his hand inside. Sandy didn't tell him he was wrong. That's not what a deep moan means.

"Relax, Sandy. Relax. It's what you wanted. You know it is. That's a nice cock. No reason to keep that a secret. Relax. Yes, yes. You're doing fine. Breathe. Don't hold it in. Relax. Go with it. Let it happen. See, there, that was good. It's done now. Don't be embarrassed. I'm flattered you wanted it that much. It's a long drive. We have plenty more time. You're young. There, see, you can start getting hard again fast. I've got a towel in my bag here. That's right, relax. You and I are going to have a real good time. Here. Feel what I've got for you."

They fucked in the dark between New York and Philadelphia. They'd already jacked each other off, and Sandy, now enthusiastic, had sucked Tab off. No one forward in the bus seemed to notice a thing. The old couple got off in New York. Six others got on, but they sat well forward—and most of them tried to go to sleep in their seats as well they could. Tab pulled Sandy over into his lap, facing the front of the bus and slowly raised and lowered him on his cock until both had ejaculated. The bandana

137

hadn't been necessary, but Tab had had to cover Sandy's mouth a couple of time, and he blessed the bus for having noisy tires.

"I've never . . ."

"I know, but you did good. And a nice tight ass."

As they approached Philadelphia, their heads together, Tab gave Sandy the lip action he knew the young man would appreciate being given to assuage his guilt for letting a stranger plow him on an intercity bus. Although Sandy had quickly given into him, his responses indicated that if he had had man-to-man experience, it hadn't been too extensive—and it certainly hadn't been like this. In time to come, though, Tab was sure that Sandy would look back at the experience and want to masturbate as he relived it—or maybe be brave enough to give in to his natural inclinations. For now, he was doing those honors for the young man for one last time.

"I never asked you your name," he murmured.

"Tab. My name is Tab Dungan."

"Dungan. That name sounds familiar."

"If you've lived in Shernhaven your whole life, it should sound familiar. My family's been there for over a hundred and fifty years. My dad owned Dungan's. It was a bar. It's called the Blue Marlin Café now. My dad was shut down fifteen years ago for serving liquor to minors, which led to a serious beat down of a guy that didn't deserve it. My dad felt real bad about that—that he never did what he should have done about it. Because it didn't end there. The guy got beat down again."

"And you came back to Shernhaven to fix that?"

"To try to. My dad's dead. But he left unfinished business—something I regretted he did—that he regretted he didn't fix. And yes, I came back to see what I could do to fix that. Now, young Mr. Sandy without a last name, we're in the Philadelphia suburbs. Can you come one more time for Mr. Fix-it?"

Even if Sandy was too exhausted to, Tab felt that the chances were good he had, indeed, fixed what had been wrong in Sandy's life too—if only temporarily. Anything he could do to counter the generations-long undertow of sexual manipulation of Shernhaven would only be to the good.

138

The Author

Habu is one of the pen names of a former supersonic spy jet pilot, intelligence agent, male model, movie actor, and diplomat. An American, he is a published mainstream novelist and short story writer under another name and in another dimension of his life, but he has written or cowritten (with Sabb) over 500 published short stories and numerous published erotica e-books, primarily of gay fiction but also memoir, straight fiction and ménage fiction. His hand and creative writing can be seen in stories and books by habu, sr71plt, shabbu, and Stephen Kessel—among unrevealed others that might surprise readers. The fictionalized GM memoir *Flying High* is loosely based on his life experiences.

BOOKS BY HABU
The Indian Prince
The Handyman
Grab Bag
Cairo Surrender
Fetish Galore!
Homeward Bound
Journey to Mirage
Choke Hold
Sporting Life